Anne McCaffrey was educ[...]
Massachusetts, and has a degree cum laude in Slavonic
Languages and Literatures. She now lives in Dublin and enjoys
riding, cooking and knitting. She is a past winner of both the
Hugo and SFWA Nebula Awards, and has written several
novels, 30 short stories and novellas, and various articles.

Anne McCaffrey

Dinosaur Planet

Futura

An Orbit Book

First published in Great Britain by
Futura Publications Limited in 1978
Fifth printing 1984

ISBN 0 8600 7948 1

Printed in Canada

Futura Publications
A Division of
Macdonald & Co (Publishers) Ltd
Maxwell House
74 Worship Street
London EC2A 2EN
A BPCC plc Company

CHAPTER ONE

Kai heard Varian's light step echoing in the empty passenger section of the shuttlecraft just as he switched off the communications unit and tripped the tape into storage.

'Sorry, Kai, did I miss the contact?' Varian came in out of breath, her suit dripping wet, carrying with her the pervasive stench of Ireta's 'fresh' air, which tainted the filtered air of the shuttle's pilot cabin. She glanced from the unlit communications panel to his face to see if he were annoyed by her tardiness, but a triumphant grin cut through her feigned penitence. 'We finally captured one of those herbivores!'

Kai had to grin in response to her elation. Varian would spend long hours tracking a creature in Ireta's damp, stinking jungles; hours of patient, obstacle-strewn search which, all too often, proved unproductive. Nevertheless, short of resorting to Discipline, Varian found it nauseatingly irksome to sit still in a comfortable chair through a Thek relay. Kai had wagered with himself that she would manage to avoid the tedious interchange with some reasonable excuse. Her news was good and her excuse valid.

'How'd you manage to capture one? Those traps you've been rigging?' he asked with genuine interest, though those same traps had taken his best mechanic from completing the seismic grid his geologists needed.

'No, not the traps,' and there was a hint of chagrin in Varian's tone. 'No, the damned fool creature was wounded and couldn't run away with the rest of the herd.' She paused to give her next statement full emphasis. 'And Kai, it bleeds blood!'

Kai blinked at her announcement. 'So?'

'Red blood!'

'Well?'

5

'Are you a biological idiot? Red blood means haemo-globin . . .'

'What's odd about that? Plenty of other species use an iron base . . .'

'*Not* on the same planet with those aquatic squirmers Tri-zein's been dissecting. *They* use a pale viscous fluid.' Varian was fleetingly contemptuous of his failure to recognize the significance. 'This planet's one mass of anomalies, biological as well as geological. No ore where you should be striking pay-dirt by the hopper-load, and me finding creatures larger than anything mentioned in text-tapes from any planet in all the systems we've explored in the last four hundred galactic stan-dard years. Of course, it may be all of a piece,' she added thoughtfully, as she pushed back the springy dark curls that framed her face.

She was tall, as so many types born on a normal-gravity planet like Earth were, with a slender but muscularly fit body which the one-piece orange ship suit displayed admirably. Despite the articles dangling from her force-screen belt, her waist was trim, and the bulges in her thigh and calf pouches did not detract from the graceful appearance of her legs.

Kai had been elated when Varian had been assigned as his co-leader. They'd been more than acquaintances on shipboard ever since she had joined the ARCT-10 as a xenob-vet, on a three galactic standard year contract. While the ARCT-10, like her sister ships in the Exploratory and Evaluation Corps, had a basic administrative and operations personnel who were ship-born and ship-bred, the complement of additional specia-lists, trainees and, occasionally, high echelon travellers for the Federated Sentient Planets changed continually, giving the ship-bred the stimulation of meeting members of other cul-tures, sub-groups, minorities and persuasions.

Kai had been attracted to Varian, first because she was an extremely pretty girl and second, because she was the opposite of Geril. He had been trying to end an unsatisfactory relation-ship with Geril, who had been so insistent that he'd had to change his quarters from the ship-born to the visitors' area of Earth-normal section of the compound ARCT-10, in order to

6

avoid her. Varian happened to be his new next-door neighbour. She was gay, bubbling with humour, and intensely interested in everything about the satellite-sized exploratory vessel. She infected him with her enthusiasm as she chivvied him into taking her on a guided tour of the various special quarters which accommodated the more esoteric sentient races of the FSP in their own atmosphere or gravity. She'd been planet-bound, Varian had told him, on how many diverse planets did not signify, so that she felt it was high time she saw how the Explorers and Evaluators lived. Especially since, she added, as a xenob-vet, she often had to correct some of EV's crazier judgments and mistakes.

Varian was a good narrator and her tales of planetary adventures, both as a youngster trailing after xenob-vet parents and as junior in the same specialty, had fascinated Kai. He'd had the usual planetary tours to combat ship-conditioned agoraphobia, and indeed had spent a whole galactic year with his mother's parents on her birthworld, but he felt his must have been dull worlds in comparison to those generating Varian's wild and amusing experiences.

Another way in which Varian excelled Geril was in her ability to argue pleasantly and effectively without losing her temper or wit. Geril had always been oppressively serious and too eager to denigrate anything of which she did not unconditionally approve. In fact, long before Kai heard that Varian was to be his co-leader, he had realized that she must have had Discipline, young as she appeared to be. He'd gone as far as to tap for a print-out of her public history from the EV's data banks. Her list of assignments had been impressive even if the public record did not give any assessment of her value on those expeditions. However, he noticed she had been promoted rapidly: this, combined with the number of assignments, indicated a young woman slated for increasing responsibility and more difficult assignments. Granted her addition to the Iretan expedition had been made almost at the last minute when life-form readings had registered on the preliminary probe, but, with her background, Ireta ought not to pose too many problems. Yet it was, as she'd said, rampant with anomalies.

'I suppose,' she was saying, 'if one has a third-generation sun with planets, one must expect oddities: like Ireta with poles hotter than its equator stinking of – I'll remember the name of that plant yet . . .'

'Plant?'

'Yes. There's a small plant, hardy enough to be grown practically anywhere on temperate Earth-type worlds, which is used in cooking. In judicious quantities, let me add,' she said with a wry grin. 'Too much of it tastes like this planet smells. Sorry, I digress. What did the Theks say?'

Kai frowned. 'Only the first reports have been picked up by our wandering Exploratory Vessel.'

Busy moping off the worst of her wetness, Varian turned to stare at him, towel suspended. 'Fardles!' She sat slowly down in the chair next to him. 'That's unnerving! Just the first?'

'That's what the Theks said . . .'

'Did you allow time enough for them to manage a reply? Scrub that question.' Varian slumped against the backrest as she added, 'Of course, *you* did,' giving him full credit for his ability to deal with the slowest moving and speaking species in the Federated System. 'That's unlike EV. They're usually so desperately greedy for initial reports, not just for the all-safe-down.'

'*My* explanation is that spatial interference . . .'

'Of course,' and Varian's face cleared of anxiety. 'That cosmic storm the next system over . . . the one the astronomers were so hairy anxious to get to . . .'

'That's what the Theks say.'

'In how many words?' asked Varian, her wry humour re-asserting itself.

The Theks were a silicate life form, like rock, extremely durable and while not immortal, certainly the closest a species had evolved towards that goal. The irreverent said that it was difficult to know a Thek elder from a rock until it spoke, but a human could perish of old age waiting for the word. Certainly the older a Thek grew and the more knowledge he acquired, the longer it took to elicit an answer from him. Fortunately for Kai, there were two young Theks on the team sent to the seventh planet of this system. One of them, Tor, Kai had known all his life. In fact, though Tor was considered young in relation to the lifespan of his species he had been on the ARCT-10 since the exploratory vessel had been commissioned one hundred and fifty galactic standard years before. Tor constantly confused Kai with his great-great-grandfather who had been an engineering officer on the ARCT-10 and whom Kai was said to resemble. It gave Kai a feeling of curious satisfaction to be on the same mission, and a planetary co-leader, with Tor. His conversation with Tor, while lengthened by space distance and Thek speech habits, was comparatively brisk.

'Tor had one word actually, Varian. Storm.' Kai added his laughter to Varian's.

'Have they ever been wrong?'

'What? Theks in error? Not in recorded history.'

'Theirs? Or ours?'

'Theirs, of course. Ours is too short. Now, about that *red* blood?'

'Well, it's not just the red blood, Kai. There are far too many unlikely coincidences. Those herbivores we've been shadowing are not only vertebrates and bleed red blood, but now that I've got close enough to have a good look, the things are pentadactyl, too.' She opened and closed her fingers at him in a clawing motion.

'Theks are pentadactyl . . . after a fashion.' Kai was well pleased they had no visual contact during the interchanges as the Theks had the unnerving habit of extruding pseudo-pods from their amorphous mass which tended to distract the viewer sometimes to the point of nausea.

'But *not* vertebrate or red-blooded. And not co-existent with another totally different life-form, like Trizein's marine squares.' Varian fumbled at the opening of her belt pouch and withdrew a flat object, well wrapped in plastic. 'It'll be interesting,' she spread the syllables out, 'to see the analysis of this blood sample.' With a graceful push she rose from the swivel chair and strode out of the pilot cabin, Kai following her.

Their boot heels echoed in the emptiness of the denuded passenger section. Its furnishings now equipped the plastic domes grouped below the shuttle in the force-screened encampment. But Trizein's work was better accomplished in the air-conditioned, ex-storage compartment which had been converted into his laboratory. A terminal to the ship's computer had been rigged up in the lab so that Trizein rarely stirred from his domain.

'So you've finally got an occupant for your corral,' Kai said.

'So I was right to plan ahead. At least we've a place big enough to stash him/it/her.'

'Don't you know which sex?'

'When you see our beast, you'll know why we haven't taken a close enough look to know.' She shuddered suddenly. 'I don't know what got to it, but whole chunks have been torn from its off flank . . . almost as if . . .' She swallowed hastily.

'As if what?'

'As if something had been feeding on it – alive.'

'What?' Kai felt his gorge rise.

'Those predators look savage enough to have done it . . . but while the creature was still living?'

The appalling concept silenced them both for several strides. A civilized diet no longer included animal flesh.

'I wonder if Tanegli's having any luck with those fruiting trees,' she said, quickly redirecting the conversation.

'D'you know if he did take the youngsters with him? I was setting up the interchange.'

'Yes,' said Varian, 'Divisti went too, so the kids are in good hands.'

'Just as well,' said Kai a little grimly, 'someone can manage them. I wouldn't relish explaining to the EV's Third Officer if anything happened to her pride and joy.'

Out of the corner of his eye, Kai saw Varian bite her lip, her eyes sparkling with suppressed amusement. It was an embarrassingly well-known fact that young Bonnard had a case of hero worship for the team's male co-leader.

'Bonnard's a good kid, Kai, and means well . . .'

'I know. I know.'

'I wonder if food tastes on this planet the way most things smell,' said Varian, again changing the subject. 'If fruit tastes of hydro-telluride . . .'

'Are we food-low?'

'No,' said Varian, who was charged by the expedition's charter to procure any additional food supplies needed. 'But Divisti is a cautious soul. The less we use of the basic subsistence supplies, the better. And fresh fruit . . . you ship-bred types may not miss it . . .'

'Landborn primates have no dietary discipline.'

They were both grinning, Varian cocking her head to one side, her grey eyes sparkling. The first day they'd met, at a table in the humanoid dining area of the huge EEC ship, they'd teased each other about dietary idiosyncrasies.

Born and brought up on the ship, Kai was used to synthesized foods, to the limited textures provided. Even when he'd been grounded for brief periods, he had never quite adjusted to the infinite variety and consistency of natural foods. Varian had boasted that she could eat anything vegetable or mineral and had found the ship's diet, even when augmented from the life support dome with freshly grown produce, rather monotonous.

'I'd call it educated tastes, man. And if the fruit tastes at all decent, you may be perverted to an appreciation of *real* food.'

Just as they reached the storage compartment, the panel shushed open and an excited man came charging towards them.

'Marvellous!' He halted mid-stride and, losing his balance, staggered against the panel wall. 'Just the people I need to see. Varian, the cell formation on those marine specimens is a real innovation. There are filaments, four different kinds . . . just take a look . . .' Trizein was pulling her back into his laboratory and gesturing urgently for Kai to follow.

11

'I've something for you, too, my friend,' and Varian extended the slide. 'We caught one of those heavy-duty herbivores, wounded, bleeding red blood . . .'

'But don't you understand, Varian,' continued Trizein, apparently deaf to her announcement, 'this is a completely *different* life form. Never in all my expeditionary experience have I come across such a cellular formation . . .'

'Nor have I come across such an anomaly as this, contrasting to your new life form.' Varian closed his fingers about the slide. 'Do be a love and run a spectro-analysis on this?'

'Red blood, you said?' Trizein blinked, changing mental gears to deal with Varian's request. He held the slide up to the light, frowned at it. 'Red blood? Isn't compatible with what I've just told you.'

At that moment, the alarm wailed its unnerving keen through the shuttle and the outside encampment and tingled jarringly at the wrist units that Kai and Varian wore as team leaders.

'Foraging party in trouble, Kai, Varian.' Paskutti's voice, his thick slurred speech unhurried, came over the intercom. 'Aerial attack.'

Kai depressed the two-way button on his wrist unit.

'Assemble your group, Paskutti. Varian and I are coming.'

'Aerial attack?' asked Varian, as both moved quickly to the iris lock of the shuttlecraft. 'From what?'

'Is the party still airborne, Paskutti?' asked Kai.

'No, sir. I have co-ordinates. Shall I call in your teams?'

'No, they'd be too far out to be useful.' To Varian he said, 'What *can* they have got into?'

'On this crazy planet? Who knows?' Varian seemed to thrive on the various alarms Ireta produced, for which Kai was glad. On his second expedition, the co-leader had been such a confirmed pessimist that the morale of the entire party had deteriorated, causing needless disastrous incidents.

As usual, the first blast of Ireta's odourous atmosphere took Kai's breath away. He'd forgotten to slip back in the deodorizing plugs he'd removed while in the shuttle. The plugs

12

helped but not when one was forced to breathe orally, as he was while running to join Paskutti's rapidly forming squad.

Though the heavy-worlders under Paskutti's direction had had farther to come, they were the first to arrive at the assembly point as Kai and Varian belted down the slope from the shuttle to the force-screen veil lock. Paskutti shoved belts, masks and stunners at the two leaders, unaware in this moment of urgency that the casual thrust of his heavy hand rocked the lighter framed people back on their heels.

Gaber, the cartographer who was emergency duty officer, came puffing down from his dome. As usual he'd forgotten to wear his force-screen belt though there was a standing order for those belts to be worn at all times. Kai'd tag Gaber for that when they got back.

'What's the emergency? I'll never get those maps drawn with all these interruptions.'

'Forage party's in trouble. Don't wander off!' said Kai.

'Oh never, Kai, never will I do anything so simplewitted, I assure you. I shan't move from the controls one centimetre, though how I'm ever to finish *my* work . . . Three days behind now and . . .'

'Gaber!'

'Yes, Kai. Yes, I understand. I really do.' The man seated himself at the veil controls glancing so anxiously from Paskutti to Varian that Kai had to nod at him reassuringly. Paskutti's heavy face was expressionless as were his dark eyes but somehow the heavy-worlder's very silence could indicate disapproval or disgust more acutely than any word he might have growled out.

Paskutti, a man in his middle years, had been in ship's security for most of his five-year tour with EEC. He had volunteered for this assignment when the call had gone through the mother ship for secondaries to assist a xenob team. Heavy-worlders often took semi-skilled tours on other worlds or on the EEC ships as the pay was extremely good; two or three tours would mean that a semi-skilled individual could earn enough credit to live the rest of his or her life in relative comfort on one of the developing worlds. Heavy-worlders were preferred as secondaries, whatever their basic specialty might be, because of their muscular strength. It was said of them that they were the muscles of humanoid FSP, generally a comment made respectfully since the heavy-worlders were not just 'muscle men' but numbered as many high ranking specialists as any other humanoid sub-group.

There was, however, no question that their sheer physical presence, the powerful legs, the compact torso, massive shoulders, weather-darkened skin, provided a visual deterrant which prompted many sentient groups to hire them as security forces, whether merely for display or as actual aggressive units. Contributing to the false notion that heavy-worlders were ill-equipped with mental abilities was the unfortunate genetic problem that, while their muscle and bone structures had altered to bear the heavy gravities, their heads had not. At first glance they did look stupid. Away from the harsh gravity and climatic conditions which bred them, heavy-worlders also had to spend a good deal of their time in heavy-grav gyms to maintain their muscular strength and to enable them to make a satisfactory adjustment when they returned to their home worlds. Perversely enough, the heavy-worlders were intensely attached to their natal worlds and most of them, having made their credit balance high enough to retire in comfort, happily returned to the cruel conditions which had developed their sub-grouping.

Paskutti and Tardma had joined the expedition out of sheer boredom with their shipboard security duties. Berru and Bakkun as geologists had been Kai's own choices since it was always good to have a few heavy-worlders on any team for the advance of their physical attributes. Both he and Varian had been pleased when Tanegli, as botanist, and Divisti, as biologist, had answered the request for such specialists.

When they had made planetfall and Varian had seen the unexpectedly big type of animal life which populated Ireta she had blessed the happenstance that there were heavy-worlders on her team. Whatever emergency they were going to meet now was approached with much more confidence in such company.

Paskutti nodded at Gaber as the cartographer's hands twitched above the veil controls. Slowly the veil lifted while Varian, by Kai's side, shuffled with impatience. One couldn't fuss Gaber by reminding him that this was an emergency and speed was essential.

Paskutti ducked under the lifting veil, charging out, the squad at his heels, before Gaber had completed the opening. It was, as usual, raining a thin mist which had been deflected, except for the heavier drops, by the main screen along with the insects small enough to be fried by contact.

They could hear Gaber muttering anxiously under his breath about people never waiting for anything as Paskutti gave the closed fist upward gesture that meant sky-trailing. The rescuers activated their lift-belts and assumed the formation assigned them by Paskutti's original briefing on emergency procedures. Kai and Varian were in the protected positions of the flying V formation.

Aloft, Kai tuned his combutton to home-in on Tanegli's signal. Paskutti gestured westward, towards the swampy lowlands and indicated speed increase as his other hand adjusted his mask.

They flew at tree top level, Kai remembering to keep his eyes horizontal, on Paskutti's back. Oddly enough his tinge of agoraphobia bothered him less in the air, so long as he didn't look directly down at the fast-moving ground. He was cushioned by the air-stream of his passage, an almost tactile support at this speed. The monotonous floor of conifers and gymnosperms which dotted this part of the continent waved briefly at their passage. High, high above, Kai caught a glimpse of circling winged monsters. Varian hadn't had a chance yet to identify or telltale any of the aerial life forms: the creatures warily made themselves scarce when the explorers were abroad in lift-belts or sleds.

They increased altitude to manoeuvre the first of the basaltic clines and then glided down the other side, skimming the endless primeval forest, its foliage in ever-varied patterns of blue-green, green and green-purple. They met the first of the thermal down-draughts and had to correct, buffeted by the air

15

currents. Paskutti signalled descent as the best solution. For him it was, with his bulk of heavy-grav-trained muscles, flesh and bone but Kai and Varian had to keep compensating with their lift-belts' auxiliary thrust jets.

As the buzz of the homer intensified Kai began to berate himself. He ought not to have allowed any exploratory groups beyond a reasonable lift-belt radius of the compound. On the other hand, Tanegli was perfectly capable of combating most of the life forms so far seen here *and* the exuberant nature of the youngsters in his charge. So what aerial trouble could they have fallen into? And so quickly. Tanegli had left in the sled just prior to Kai's scheduled contact with the Theks. They could barely have made their destination before coming afoul of whatever it was. Tanegli would surely have mentioned any casualty. Then Kai wondered if the sled had been damaged. They'd only the one big unit, and the four two-man sleds for his seismic teams. The smaller sleds could, at a pinch, take four passengers, but no equipment.

The land dropped away again and they corrected their flight line. Far in the purple distance the first range of volcanoes could be seen on the edge of the inland sea; a lake that was doomed to be destroyed by the restless tectonic action of this very active world. That was the first area he'd had tested for its seismicity because he'd worried that perhaps their granite shelf might be too close to tectonic activity and turn mobile. But the first print-out of the cores had been reassuring. The lake would subside, probably giving way to small hills pushed up from beneath, clad with sediment and eventually folded under, for this was the near edge of the stable continental shelf on which the encampment had been placed.

The steamy, noxiously scented heat of the swamplands began to rise to meet them: cloying humidity intensified the basic hydro-telluride stench. The homer's buzz grew louder and became continuous.

Kai was not the only member of the party scanning ahead. Far-sighted Paskutti saw the sled first, in a grove of angiosperms, parked on a sizable hummock that jutted into the swamp, away from the firmer mass of the jungle. The great purple-barked, many-rooted branches of the immense trees, well-scarred by herbivorous assaults, were untenanted by avian life, and Kai was beginning to feel the anger of relief overcome concern.

Paskutti's arm gesture caught his attention and he followed the line of the heavy-worlder's sweep towards the swamp. Several tan objects were slowly being dragged under the water by the pointed snouts of the swamp-dwellers. A minor battle began as two long-necked denizens contended for the possession of one corpse. The victor claimed the spoils by the simple expedient of sitting on the body and sinking with it into the muddy waters.

Tardma, the heavy-worlder directly in front of Kai, pointed in the other direction, toward the firmer land, where a winged creature obviously recovering from a stun blast, was swaying upright.

Paskutti fired a warning triplet and then motioned the group to land on the inland side of the grove. They came to a running stop, the heavy-worlders automatically deploying towards the swamp since the likelihood of attack was from that quarter. Kai, Varian and Paskutti jogged towards the sled from behind which the foragers now emerged.

Tanegli stood waiting, his squat solid bulk a bastion around which the smaller members of the party ranged: the three youngsters, Kai was relieved to see, appeared to be all right, as did the zeno-botanist Divisti. Now Kai noticed the small pile of assorted brilliant yellow objects in the storage cage of the sled: more of similar shape and colour were strewn about the clear ground of the small grove.

'We called prematurely,' said Tanegli by way of greeting. 'The swamp creatures proved curious allies.' He replaced his stunner in his belt and dusted his thick hands as if dismissing the incident.

'What was attacking you?' Varian asked, staring about her.

'These?' asked Paskutti as he dragged a limp, furred and winged creature from behind the trunk of a thick tree.

'Watch out!' said Tanegli, reaching to his belt before he saw the stunner in Paskutti's. 'I set the gun on a light charge.'

'It's one of those gliders. See, no socket for the wing to fold,' Varian said, ignoring the protests of the heavy-worlders as she moved the limp wings out and back.

Kai eyed the pointed beak of the creature with apprehension, suppressing an irrational desire to step back.

'Carrion eater by the size and shape of that jaw,' remarked Paskutti, peering with considerable interest.

'Well and truly stunned,' Varian said with a final twitch of arrangement to the wings. 'What was dead enough to attract it here?'

'That!' Tanegli pointed to the edge of the clearing, to a mottled brown bundle, its belly swelling up out of the course vegetation.

'And I rescued this!' said Bonnard, stepping clear of his friends so that Kai and Varian saw the small replica of the dead animal in his arms. 'But it didn't bring the gliders. They were already here. It's very young. And its mother is dead now.'

'We found it over there, hiding in the roots of the tree,' said Cleiti, loyally supporting her friend, Bonnard, against adult disapproval.

'The sled must have alarmed the gliders,' said Tanegli, taking up the story, 'driven them away from her. Once we had landed and started collecting the fruit, they returned.' He shrugged his wide shoulders.

Varian was examining the shivering little creature, peering into its mouth, checking its feet. She gave a little laugh. 'Anomaly time again. Perissodactyl feet and herbivorous teeth. There's a good fellow. Nice to have something your own size, isn't it, Bonnard?'

'Is it all right? It just shivers,' Bonnard's face was solemn with worry.

'I'd shiver too if I got picked up by huge things that didn't smell right.'

'Then perisso . . . whatever it is, isn't dangerous?'

Varian laughed and ruffled Bonnard's short cropped hair. 'No, just a way of classifying it. Perissodactyl means uneven numbered toes. I want a look at its mother.' Careful of the

18

nearby sword plants with their deceptively decorative purple leaves, she made her way towards the dead creature. A long low whistle broke from her lips. 'I suppose it's possible,' she said in a sympathetic tone of voice. 'Well, her leg's broken. That's what made her fair game to the scavengers.'

A loud noise attracted everyone's attention; an ominous sucking sound. From the swamp a huge head and neck broke the slimy surface and wavered in their direction.

'We could be considered fair game, too, by such as that,' said Kai. 'Let's get out of here.'

Paskutti frowned at the great and evil looking head, fingering his stunner onto the strongest setting. 'That creature would require every charge we have to stop it.'

'We came for fruit . . .' Divisti said, pointing to the litter in the clearing. 'They *look* viable, and fresh food would do us all good,' she added with as wistful a tone as Kai had ever heard from a heavy-worlder.

'I'd say we had a safety factor of about ten minutes before that swamp creature's brain can make the logical assumption that we're edible,' said Tanegli, as unconcerned as ever by physical threat. He began to gather up the scattered thick-skinned fruits and toss them into the storage cage of the six-man sled.

In point of fact, those sleds had been known to lift twenty, a capability never mentioned in the designers' specifications. The exploratory sled was an all-purpose vehicle, its ultimate potential not yet realized. High-sided and slightly more than eight metres long with a closed deck forward for storage, its compact engine and power pack under the rear loading space, the vessel could be fitted with comfortable seating for six as well as the pilot and co-pilot, with the storage cage, as it was now. When the seating was removed or lashed to the deck, a sled could carry enormous weight, on board or attached to the powerful winches fore, aft and midships on either side. The plascreen could be retracted into the sides or raised in sections. The sled had both retro and forward jets with a vertical lift ability which could be used in defence or emergency flight. The two-man sleds were smaller replicas of the big one and had the advantage of being easily dismantled and stored: in flight, usually in the larger vehicle.

Augmented by the rescue squad, the foragers accumulated enough fruit to fill the sled's storage cage in the time it took more carrion eaters to begin spiralling above the grove. The swamp head seemed mesmerized by the comings and goings of the group, swinging slowly back and forth.

'Kai, we don't have to leave him here, do we?' asked Bonnard, with an apprehensive Cleiti by his side. He had the orphan in his arms.

'Varian? Any use to you?'

'Certainly. I'd no intention of leaving it. It's a relief not to have to chase something over the continent to get a close look.' She frowned at the suggestion of abandonment. 'Into the sled with you, Bonnard. Keep a hold on it. Cleiti, you sit on his right, I'll sit left. There we are. Belt up.'

The others stood back as Tanegli took off in the sled, gliding indolently over the ooze and the undecided beast that still regarded the grove with unblinking interest.

'Set for maximum stun,' Paskutti told them, glancing overhead. 'Those carrion are coming in again.'

Even as the rescuers lifted from the ground, Kai saw the carrion fliers circling downwards, their heads always on the dead creature in the grass below. Kai shuddered. The dangers of space, instant and absolute, were impersonal and the result of breaking immutable laws. The deadly intent of these things held a repulsively personal malevolence that disturbed him profoundly.

CHAPTER TWO

Rain and head winds buffeted the airborne V so steadily on their way back that the heavily powered sled had long since landed when Kai and the heavy-worlders finally set foot in the compound. Varian and the three children were busy constructing a small run for the orphan.

'Lunzie's trying to deduce a diet,' Varian told Kai.

'Just what is its anomalous state?'

'Against every odd in the galaxy, we have succoured a young mammal. At least its mother had teats. It's not very old, born rather mature, you see, able to walk and run almost at birth . . .'

'Did you . . .'

'Debug it? Externally yes. Had to or we'd all be hosting parasites. I've interrupted more of Trizein's carefully scheduled work to run a tissue sample on it so we can figure out what proteins it must have in its diet. It's got some growing to do to reach momma's size. Not that she was very large.'

Kai looked down at the tiny creature's red-brown furred body: a very unprepossessing creation, he thought, with no redeeming feature apart from wistful eyes to endear it to anyone other than its own mother. But, remembering the waving swamp-dweller's head, and the hungry malice in the circling scavengers' relentless approach, he was glad they'd brought the thing in. And it might occupy Bonnard and keep the boy from following him everywhere.

Kai stripped off his belt and face mask, rubbing at the strap marks. He was tired after the return trip. The heavy-worlders had immense resources of stamina but Kai's ship-trained muscles ached from the exertions of the morning.

'Say, don't we have to contact the Ryxi, too?' Varian asked, glancing at her wrist recorder and tapping the reddened 1300 that meant a special time.

Kai grinned his thanks for the reminder and made for the

21

shuttlecraft with a fair display of energy. There was still a lot of busy day ahead of him. He'd get a pepper to pick his energy level up, and he'd get a bit of a breather while he made contact with the avians. Then he had to go see that complex of coloured lakes Berru had documented yesterday in her sweep south. He found it damned odd there were no more than traces of the normal metals you'd think would be in abundance everywhere on this untouched planet. Coloured waters indicated mineral deposits. He only hoped the concentrations were heavy enough to make them worthwhile. There ought to be something in old fold mountains, if only some tin or zinc and copper. They'd found ore-minerals but no deposits worth the name.

Kai's orders from Exploratory and Evaluation Corps were to locate and assay the mineral and metallurgical potential of this planet. And Ireta, a satellite of a suspected third generation sun, ought to be rich in the heavier elements, rich in the neptunium, plutonium and the more esoteric of the rare transuranics and actinites above uranium on the periodic table, so urgently and constantly required by the Federation of Sentient Populations the search for which was one of the primary tasks of the EEC.

The diplomatic might say that EEC was exploring the galaxy, seeking to bring within its sphere of influence all rational sentient beings, augmenting the eighteen peace-loving species already incorporated in the FSP. But the search for energy was the fundamental drive. The diversity of its member species gave the Federation the ability to explore more types of planets, but colonization was incidental to exploitation.

The three useful planets of the sun Arrutan had long been marked on star charts as promising but only recently had the Executive Council decided to mount the present three-part expedition. Kai had heard the whisper that it was because the Theks wished to be included. This whisper was partially substantiated during his private conference with the EEC Chief Officer on board the exploratory vessel ARCT-10. The CO had privily informed Kai that the Thek had superior control of the three teams, and he was to consider himself under their orders if they chose to supersede him. Vrl, the Ryxi team leader, had been given the same orders, but everyone knew the Ryxi. And it was common knowledge that having a Thek on a team spelled ultimate success: Theks were dependable, Theks were thorough, the ultimate altruists. The cynics replied that altruism was easy when a creature calculated its life span in thousands of years. The Theks had elected to be placed on the seventh world of the primary, a heavy metals, heavy gravity planet, exactly suited to Theks.

The light-cored planet, fifth from the sun Arrutan, with a low gravity and temperate climate, was being evaluated by the Ryxi, an aerial species, who were in critical need of new planets to relieve their population pressure and give industry and opportunity to the restless young.

Kai's assignment, the fourth planet in the system, exhibited curious anomalies. Originally designated a second generation sun, with elements up to the transuranic, Arrutan patently did not conform to that classification. A probe sent out for a preliminary survey registered that the fourth planet was undeniably ovoid in shape; the poles were hotter than the equator: the seas registered warmer than the land mass which covered the northern pole. There was an almost constant rainfall, and an inshore wind of variable velocities up to full gale force. An axial tilt of some fifteen degrees had been postulated. The readings indicated life forms in water and on land. A xenobiological team was added to the geological.

Kai had requested a remote sensor to locate the ore concentrations but at that point the storm in the next system had been sighted and he found his request very low on the priority list. He was told that the original probe tapes would give him ample information to locate metal and mineral, and to get the job done *in situ*. Right now ARCT-10 had an unparalleled opportunity to observe free matter in action.

Kai took the official brush-off in good part. What he did object to was having the youngsters dumped on his hands at the last minute. To his complaint that this was a working expedition, not a training exercise, he was told that the ship-born must have sufficient planetary experiences early in their lives to overcome the danger of conditional agoraphobia. The hazard was not lightly to be dismissed by the ship-born: useless to explain to the planet-bred. But Kai railed against the expediency that made his team the one to expand the horizons of three members who were only half into their second decades. This planet was exceedingly active, volcanically and tectonically, and dangerous for ship-bred juveniles. The two girls, Cleiti and Terilla, were biddable and no trouble until Bonnard, the son of the Third Officer of the EV, instigated all manner of hazard-strewn games.

The very first day, while Kai and his team were dropping cores around the landing site to be sure they had landed on the more stable continental shield, Bonnard had gone 'exploring' and lacerated a protective suit because he hadn't remembered to activate the force-field. He had stumbled into the sword plant, as pretty as the harmless decorative plants in the EV's conservatory but able to slice flesh and suit to ribbons with the most negligible of contacts. There had been other incidents during the nine days the party had been landed. While the other team members seemed to make light of the boy's escapades and were amused by his adoration of Kai, the team-leader sincerely hoped the little orphaned beast would divert Bonnard.

Kai took a long sip of the pepper, its tart freshness soothing his nerves as well as his palate. He glanced down at his recorder, switched on the comunit, arranged the recording equipment to the speed necessary to slow the Ryxi speech pattern into understandable tones for later review. He could generally keep up with their rippingly fast voices but a tape helped to resolve any questions.

Kai had been designated the liaison officer between the two groups. He had the patience and tact required for dealing with the slow Thek, and the ear and wit to keep up with the quick aerial Ryxi who could never have communicated with the Thek, and with whom the Thek preferred not to bother.

Right on time the Ryxi leader, Vrl, made the contact, trilling out the courtesies. Kai relayed the information that only the first reports from each of the teams had been picked up by the EV, and gave his assumption that the spatial storm viewed before the exploratory groups had left the ship must be causing sufficient interference to prevent a pick-up of other reports.

Vrl, politely slowing his speech to a rate which must have been frustrating to him, said that he wasn't worried; that was for the Slows to fret about. Vrl's first report was the important one for his people: it confirmed the initial probe analysis that this planet contained no indigenous intelligent life form and could adequately support his race. Vrl was forwarding by interplanetary drone a full report for Kai's interest. Vrl ended by saying that all were in good health and full feather. Then he asked what winged life had been observed on Ireta.

Kai told him, speaking as fast as he could get the words past his teeth, that they had observed several aerial life forms from a distance and would investigate further when possible. He refrained from naming one form as the scavengers they were but promised, at Vrl's liquidly trilled request, to forward a full tape when completed. The Ryxi as a species had one gross sin: they hated to think that another aerial life form might one day challenge their unique position in FSP. This prejudice was one reason why Ryxi were not often included in EV complements. The other valid reason was that Ryxi fretted in enclosed spaces to the point of suicide. Very few bothered to qualify for Exploratory Services since they were so psychologically ill-suited to the life. Necessity had forced them into this mission and most of the members had spent the journey time in cryonic suspension. Vrl had been awakened two ship weeks before touchdown to be apprised of the necessary routine of report and contact with the other two sections. While Vrl, like all his ilk, was an interesting creature, vital, flamboyant with his plumage and personality, Kai and Varian were relieved to have the Theks along as balance.

'Did Vrl remember to be there?' asked Varian, entering the control cabin.

'Yes, and all's well with him, though he's mighty curious about winged life here.'

'They always are, those jealous feathers!' Varian made a face. 'I remember a deputation from Ryxi at University on Chelida. They wanted to vivisect those winged tree Rylidae from Eridani 5.'

Kai suppressed a sympathetic shudder. He wasn't surprised. The Ryxi were known to be bloody-minded. Look at their courtship dance – males armed with leg spurs and the victor usually *killing* his opponent. You couldn't quite excuse that on the grounds of survival of the fittest. You didn't have to kill to improve the genotype.

'Is there another pepper going? I've been trying to keep up with my team mates.' She slid into the chair.

Kai snorted at that folly and handed her a container of stimulant, chuckling.

'I know we don't have to keep up with the heavy-worlders,' Varian said with a groan, 'and I know that they know that we can't, but *I* can't help *trying*!'

'It's frustrating. I know.'

'So do I. Oh, Trizein says the little creature is indeed a mammal and will need a lactoprotein, heavy in calcium, glucose, salt and a good dollop of phosphates.'

'Can Divisti and Lunzie whomp something up?'

'Have done. Bonnard is feeding . . . or I should say, attempting to feed Dandy.'

'It's named already?'

'Why not? It certainly isn't programmed to answer a meal call – yet.'

'Intelligent?'

'Of a restricted sort. It's already programmed to a certain number of instinctive responses, being born fairly mature.'

'Is that herbivore of yours mammalian?'

'Nooooo . . .'

'What's the yes in that no for?'

'Granted that viviparous and oviparous types often co-exist on a planet . . . and that you'd get some very odd gene specialization to cope with environment here, but I cannot rationalize that aquatic life cell formation with Dandy or with that big herbivore.

'And speaking of that beast, Trizein says its cell structure is remarkably familiar; he's going to do an in-depth comparison. In the meantime, I've his okay to use a CHCL₃ gas on it so we can dress those wounds before they turn septic. Can we rig a force-screen arc over that corral we erected so the wound can be kept free of blood-sucking organisms while it heals?' When Kai nodded, she continued. 'And would you also ask your core teams to keep an eye out for any scavengers circling? Whatever wounded the herbivore probably attacks other animals. One, I'd like to know what kind of predator is that savage to its prey; and two, there's always a chance that we can find amenable specimens by saving their lives. They're so much easier to capture when they're too weak to struggle or run.'

'Aren't we all? I'll give the word to my teams. Only don't make this compound a veterinary hospital, will you, Varian? We don't have the space.'

'I know, I know. Those that are large enough to fend for themselves go into the corral anyhow.'

They rose, both revived by the peppers. But their brief respite in the conditioned air of the shuttle made that first step outside a gasper.

'Man is an adaptable creature,' Kai told himself under his breath, 'flexible, comprehending his universe, a high survival type. But did we have to get a planet that reeks?'

'Can't win 'em all, Kai,' said Varian with a laugh. 'And I find this place fascinating.' She left him standing in the open lock.

The rain had stopped, Kai noticed, at least for the moment. The sun peered through the cloud cover, getting ready to steam bake them for a while. With the cessation of rain, Ireta's insect battalions once more flung themselves against the force-screen that arched above the compound. Blue sparks erupted as the smaller creatures were incinerated, glowing blue where larger organisms were stunned by the charge.

He gazed out over the compound, experiencing a certain sense of accomplishment. Behind him, and above the compound itself, was the tough ceramic-hulled shuttlecraft, twenty-one metres long, with its nose cone blackened by the friction heat of entering Ireta's atmosphere. Its stubby glide wings were retracted now, leaving it slightly ovoid in shape, the central portion being larger than either end. From its top blossomed the communications spire and the homing device that would guide in its children-sleds. Unlike early models of the compound-ship to planet shuttle, most of the vessel was cargo and passenger space since the incredibly efficient, Thek-designed power packs which utilized an established isotope were compact and no longer took up the bulk of the shuttle's interior. An additional benefit of the Thek power pack was that lighter weight ships, which had the specially developed ceramic hulls, could deliver the same payload as the structurally reinforced titanium hulled vessels, needed for the anti-quated fission and fusion drives.

The shuttle rested on a shelf of granite which, spreading out and down, formed a shallow amphitheatre, roughly four hundred metres in diameter. Varian had pointed out that the shuttle's first touch-down had been smack in the middle of some animal route, to judge by the well trampled dirt. Kai had not needed any urging to change site. Open vistas might give you a chance to assess visitors but it was a bit much for his ship-trained eyes.

Force-screen posts surrounded the present encampment in which temporary living, sleeping and working domes had been erected. Water, tapped from an underground source, had to be softened and filtered. Even so, those like Varian, who were less used to recycled water which always tasted faintly of chemicals, grumbled about its mineral flavour.

Divisti and Trizein had tested several forms of Iretan vegetation and succulents, finding them safe for human consumption. Divisti and Lunzie had collaborated and produced a pulp from the greenery that might be nutritionally correct but had such a nauseating taste and curious consistency that only the heavy-worlders would eat it. They were known to eat anything. Even, it was rumoured, animal flesh.

Nonetheless, for the short time they'd been on Ireta, Kai was pleased with their accomplishments. The camp was securely situated in a protected position, on a stable shield land mass composed of basement rock that tested out 3000 MY. There was an ample water supply and an indigenous resource of synthesizable food to hand.

A faint uneasiness nagged at him suddenly. He wished that the EV had stripped more reports from the satellite beamer. It was probably nothing more than interference from that spatial storm. The EV, having established that all three expeditions were functioning, might have no reason to strip the beamer for a while. It would be back this way in a hundred days or so. This was a routine expedition. So was the EV's interest in the storm. Unless, of course, the EV had run into the Others.

Peppers made you hyper-imaginative as well as energetic, Kai told himself firmly as he started down the incline to the floor of the compound. The 'Others' were a myth, made up to frighten bad children, or childlike adults. While occasionally EEC units found dead planets and passed likely systems interdicted on the charts for no ostensible reason though their planets would certainly have been suitable to one or another member of the Federation . . .

Kai became angry with himself and, forcing down such reflections, tramped through the alien dust to Gaber's dome.

The cartographer had returned to his patient translating of taped recordings to the master chart, over which the probe photos were superimposed. As Kai's teams brought more detailed readings, Gaber updated the appropriate grid and removed the photo. At the moment, the tri-d globe looked scabrous. In the other half of dome was the seismic screen which Portegin was setting up. Glancing quickly past it, Kai thought Portegein was loosing his knack: the screen was on and registering far too many core points, some barely visible.

'I'm days behind myself. I told you that, Kai,' said Gaber, his aggrieved tone somewhat counterbalanced by a rueful smile. He straightened, twisting his neck to relieve taut muscles. 'And I'm glad you've come because I cannot work with Portegin's screen. He says it's finished but you can see it's not functioning correctly.'

Gaber swung his gimballed chair about and pointed his inking pen at the core monitor screen.

Kai gave a closer look and then began to fiddle with the manual adjustments.

'You see what I mean? Echoes! And then faint responses where I know perfectly well your teams have not had a chance to lay cores. Here in the south and the south-east . . .' Gaber was taping the screen with his pen. 'Unless, of course, your teams are duplicating efforts . . . but the readings would be clearer. So I have to assume that the machine itself is malfunctioning.'

Kai barely attended to Gaber's complaints. In his belly a coldness formed, a coldness that had to do with thinking about the Others. But, if it had been the Others who laid the faintly responding cores, then this planet would have been interdicted. One thing was positive in Kai's mind : his teams had not set those other lights, nor duplicated work.

'That is interesting, Gaber,' he replied with a show of an indifference he was far from feeling. 'Obviously from an older survey. This planet's been in the EEC library for a long time, you know. And cores are virtually indestructible. See here, in the north, where the fainter cores leave off? That's where the plate action had deformed the land mass into those new fold mountains.'

'Why didn't we have those old records? Of course, a prior survey would account for why we haven't found anything more than traces of metal and mineral deposits here.' Gaber meant the continental shield. 'But why under a logical regime no mention is made of a previous seismic history, I simply cannot understand.'

'Oh, it is old, and probably got erased for modern programs. A computer does not have an infinite capacity for data storage.'

Gaber snorted. 'Scorching odd, I call it, to send down an expedition without the full facts at their disposal.'

'Perhaps, but it'll cut down on our time here : some of our work's already done,'

'Cut down our time here?' Gaber gave a derisive laugh. 'Not likely.'

Kai turned slowly to stare at the man. 'What maggot's in your mind now, Gaber?'

Gaber leaned forward, despite the fact the two men were alone in the dome. 'We could have been . . .' he hesitated affectedly, '. . . planted!'

'Planted?' Kai let out a shout. 'Planted? Just because the seismic shows old cores here?'

'Wouldn't be the first time the victims weren't told.'

'Gaber, we've got the Third Officer's beloved and only offspring with us. We'll be picked up.'

Gaber remained obdurate.

'There'd be no point in planting us. Besides, what about the Ryxi and the Theks.'

Gaber snorted scornfully. 'The Theks don't care how long they stay anywhere. They live practically forever, and the Ryxi were to plant anyhow, weren't they? And it isn't *just* those cores that convince me. I've thought so a long time – ever since I knew we had a xenobiologist and heavy-worlders with us.'

'Gaber!' Kai spoke sharply enough to startle the older man, 'you will not mention planting to me again, nor to anyone else in this expedition. That is an order!'

'Yes, sir. I'm sure it is, sir.'

'Further, if I find you without your belt one more time . . .'

'Sir, it pokes me in the gut when I'm bending over the board.' But Gaber was hurriedly fastening on the force-screen belt.

'Leave the belt slack, then, and turn the buckle to one side, but wear it! Now, bring your recorder and some fresh tapes. I want to recon those lakes Berru charted . . .'

'That was only yesterday, and as I told you I am three days behind . . .'

'All the more reason for us to check those lakes out personally. I've got to show some progress in my next report to EV on deposits. And . . .' Kai tapped out a code, waiting impatiently at the terminal for the print-out on the mysterious core sites, 'we'll do a ground check on a couple of these.'

'Well, now, it'll be good to get away from the board. I haven't done any field work yet on this expedition,' said Gaber, pressing closed his jumpsuit fastenings. He reached for the recording unit and tape blanks which he distributed in leg pouches.

His tone was so much brighter and less dour and foreboding that Kai wondered if he'd been unfair to keep the man continually in the dome. Could that be why Gaber had come up with the astounding notion that they'd been planted. Too little action narrowed perceptions.

But Gaber, as witness his laxity over the belt, was so narding absentminded that he was more of a liability than the youngest youngster in the landing party. As Kai recalled, Gaber's credentials rated him as ship-bred, having made only four expeditions in his six decades. This would likely be the last if Kai made an honest report of his efficiency. Unless, the insidious thought plagued Kai, they had indeed been planted. Better than most leaders, Kai knew how undermining such a rumour could be. Yes, it would be better to keep Gaber so fully occupied that he had no time for reflection.

Kai did, however, have to remind Gaber to strap himself into the sled seat, which the cartographer did with profuse apologies.

'I do wish I'd been born a Thek,' said Gaber, while Kai checked the sled's controls and energy levels. 'To live long enough to watch the evolution of a world..Ah, what an opportunity!'

Kai chuckled. 'If they're not too involved with thinking to look around in time.'

'They never forget a thing they've seen or heard.'

'How could one tell? It takes a year to carry on any sort of a dialogue with an Elder.'

'You young people can only think of quick returns. Not end results. It's end results which count. Over the course of my years on ARCT-10, I've had many meaningful chats with Theks. The older ones, of course.'

'Chats? How long a lag between sentences?'

'Oh, not long. We'd scheduled replies on a once a ship week basis. I found it extremely stimulating to formulate the most information in the fewest phrases.'

'Oh, I'll grant the Theks are past masters at the telling phrase.'

'Why, even a single word can have unusual significance when uttered by a Thek,' Gaber went on with unexpected volubility. 'When you can appreciate fully that each Thek holds within its brain the total knowledge of its own forebears, and can distill this infinite wisdom in single succinct words or phrases . . .'

'No perspective . . .' Kai was concentrating on lifting the sled out of the compounds.

'I beg your pardon?' Gaber's apology was more of a reprimand.

'Their wisdom is Thek wisdom and is not readily applicable to our human conditions.'

'I never implied that it was. Or should be.' Gaber was distinctly annoyed with Kai.

'No, but wisdom should be relevant. Knowledge is something else, but not necessarily distilled from wisdom.'

'My dear Kai, *they* understand reality, not just the illusion of a very brief and transitory lifespan such as ours.'

The telltale, as sensitive to thermal readings as to movement of any object larger than a man's fist, rattled, informing the two men that they were passing over living creatures, at that moment hidden from their eyes by the thick vegetation. The rattle turned into a purr as the sensitive recorder indicated that the life form had already been tagged with the telltale indelible paint with which the various scouting teams marked any beasts they observed.

'Life form . . . no telltale,' exclaimed Gaber as the rattle occurred after a short interval of silence.

Kai altered his course in the direction of the cartographer's finger. 'And moving from us at a fast rate.' Gaber leaned across to the windboard to check the telltagger, nodding to Kai to indicate it was ready and set.

'Maybe it's one of those predators Varian's been trying to catch,' Kai said. 'Herbivores go about in groups. Hang on, there's a break in the jungle ahead of us. It can't possibly swerve.'

'You're directly over it,' Gaber said, his voice rough with excitement.

Both beast and airborne sled reached the small clearing simultaneously. But, as if it recognized the danger of an open space with an unknown enemy above it, the beast was a bare flash, a stretched and running mottled body, ending in a stiffly held long tail: all the retinal after-image Kai retained.

'Got it!' Gaber's triumphant yell meant the creature had been telltagged. 'I've film on it, too. The speed of the thing.'

'I think it's one of Varian's predators.'

'I don't believe herbivores are capable of such bursts of speed. Why, it outdistanced this sled.' Gaber sounded amazed. 'Are we following it?'

'Not today. But it's tagged. Enter the grid co-ordinates, will you, Gaber? Varian's sure to want to come look-see. That's one of the first predators we've been able to telltag. Luck, sheer luck, coming over that clearing.'

Kai veered back to his original course, slightly north, towards the first body of water that Berru had sighted. It ought to be near the inland sea which was shown on the satellite pictures.

Reality, thought Kai, echoing Gaber. Now the satellite photos had been theoretical, in one sense, since they'd had to be shot through the ever-present cloud cover, while Kai, by flying over the depicted terrain, was the reality, the direct experience. Kai could appreciate the essence of Gaber's comment: what an incredible experience it would be to watch this planet evolve, to see the land masses tortured and rent by quake, shift, fault, deformation and fold. He sighed. In his mind, he speeded up the process like the quickly flipped frames of single exposure prints. It was hard for short-lived man to comprehend the millions of years, the billions of days that it took to form continents, mountains, rivers, valleys. And clever as a geophysicist might be in predicting change, such realities as geophysics had been able to observe in its not so lengthy history always exceeded projections.

Gaber's life-instrument beeped constantly now, and with no counter burr from the telltale they diverted again, this time to tag a large herd of tree-eaters.

'Don't recall pics of monsters like that before,' Kai told Gaber as they circled round the creatures, now partially visible through the sparse forest cover. 'I want to get a good look. Set the camera and the telltale, Gaber. I'm coming around. Hang on.'

Kai turned the air sled, braking speed as he matched the forward motion of the lumbering beasts. 'Scorch it, but they're the biggest things I've seen yet!'

'Keep up,' Gaber cried in nervous excitement for Kai was skimming very low. 'Those necks are powerful.' The beasts had very long necks, mounted on massive shoulders which were supported by legs the size of tree stumps.

'Necks may be powerful but the brains aren't,' said Kai. 'And their reaction time is double slow.' The beasts were looking back towards the direction in which Kai had first approached them. Several had not even registered the alien's appearance at all but continued to strip trees as they passed. 'Gigantic herbivores, foraging even as they move. They must account for half a forest a day.'

One of the long-necked creatures neatly bit off the crown of a cycad and continued its lumbering progress with huge fronds dripping from its not too capacious mouth. A smaller member of the herd obligingly took up one trailing frond and munched on that.

'Heading towards the water?' Kai asked, impressed as well as appalled by the dimensions of the animals. He heard the tagger spit.

'There does seem to be a well-travelled lane through the vegetation. I tagged most of them.' Gaber patted the muzzle of the tag gun.

Kai tilted the sled so he could observe the beasts. Ahead, and down a long incline, lay the shimmering waters of one of Berru's lakes. Kai took the transparency of the probe print and laid it over the replica of scale map which Gaber had been patiently drawing from the data of Kai's teams.

'We should have the precipice on our right, Gaber. Adjust your face-mask to distance vision and see if you can spot it.'

Gaber peered steadily across the distance. 'Cloudy, but you ought to change course by about five degrees.'

They flew over terrain that gradually became more and more swamp-like until water replaced land entirely. At this point a definite shoreline appeared, rising first into small bluffs of well-weathered grey stone which gave way to sheer cliffs rising several hundred metres in an ancient transform fault. Kai ascended and the passage of the sled alarmed cliff dwellers into flight, bringing an exclamation of surprised delight from Gaber.

'Why, they're golden! And furred!'

Kai, remembering the vicious heads of the scavengers, veered hastily from their flight path.

'They're following us,' cried Gaber, unperturbed.

Kai glanced over his shoulder. As far as he knew, scavengers only attacked the dying or dead. Judiciously he applied more air speed. The sled could easily outdistance them.

'They're still following us.'

Kai shot a glance over his shoulder. No question of it, the golden avians were following but maintaining a discreet distance, and different levels. Even as Kai watched, the fliers changed positions, as if each wanted to see various aspects of the intruder. Again Kai loaded on more speed. So did the fliers, without apparently expending much effort.

'I wonder how fast they do fly?'

'Are they dangerous, do you suppose?' asked Gaber.

'Possibly, but I'd say that this sled is too big for them to attack, singly or with the numbers they have behind us now. I must bring Varian to see them. And tell the Ryxi.'

'Why ever tell them? They couldn't fly in this heavy atmosphere.'

'No, but Vrl asked me about Ireta's aerial life. I'd hate to tell him there were only scavengers.'

36

'Oh, yes, quite. I agree. Merciful gods, look below to your left.'

They were well over the water now, stained red by the mineral content of the rocks which bordered it and its watershed. Clearly visible was the plant strewn bottom which shelved off slightly into murky brownness and considerable depth, according to Kai's instrumentation. From out of that depth a great body torpedoed, responding to the shadow cast by the sled. Kai had a startled impression of a blunt head, grey-blue shining skin, and too many rows of sharp yellow-white teeth, needle sharp. He heard Gaber's startled cry of horror. Instinctively he slammed on the emergency drive. And corrected hurriedly as they sped uncomfortably close to the curving cliffs.

Looking back, Kai saw only the rippling circles of the monster's exit and entry on the surface, circles converging together over the twenty-five metres of its jump. He gulped and swallowed against a dryness in his throat. As if that attack had been a signal, more aquatic denizens leapt and dove, and other battles began under and on the surface of the water.

'I think,' Gaber's stammer was pronounced, 'that we started something.'

'Well, they can finish it,' said Kai as he turned the blunt nose of the sled.

'The golden fliers are still following us,' Gaber said after a few moments. 'They're closing.'

Kai spared a backward glance and saw the first rank of fliers moving steadily abreast of the sled, their heads turned towards himself and Gaber.

'Go away,' Gaber said, standing up and waving both arms towards the birds. 'Go away. Don't get too close. You'll get hurt!'

Half-amused, half-concerned, Kai watched the creatures swing away from Gaber's flapping. They also maintained their forward speed and their inspection.

'We're surrounded by them, Kai,' and Gaber's tone took on a worried note.

'If they were dangerous, they'd've had plenty of time to

attack, I think. But let's just lose the escort. Sit down, Gaber, and hang on!' Kai hit the jet accelerator again, and abruptly left the fliers in the heat haze as the sled flung forward. There couldn't have been any expression on the golden faces, but Kai had the distinct impression that they'd been astonished by the sudden speed.

He must ask Varian what degree of intelligence was possible in these apparently primitive life forms. The Ryxi were not the only winged species in the galaxy but very few avian species were highly intelligent. Capability seemed to have a direct ratio to the amount of time spend on the ground.

Whatever life form would dominate on this planet was thousands of years away from emerging. That didn't keep Kai from wishful thinking and speculation. It would be nice to see the Ryxi superceded.

'Did you get some good tapes of them?' Kai asked Gaber as he reduced speed to cruising. No use wasting more power than necessary.

'Oh yes, indeed I did,' Gaber said, patting the recorder. 'You know, Kai, I think they showed considerable intelligence.' He sounded astonished.

'We'll get Varian to give an opinion. She's the expert.' Kai turned the sled to the coordinates of the nearest echo-core. Varian might have some biological puzzles but he now had another geological one.

Despite what he'd said so nonchalantly to Gaber, the unexpected materialization of those cores unnerved him. Yes, this plant and the system had been in the computer bank, but surely there would have been some indication if it had been surveyed. A previous survey, however, would account for the lack of ore-deposit on these old mountains. The first party would have mined the shield area, and quite likely whatever other likely land mass, or seas, had been workable; land which had long since been rolled under in subsequent plate activity. Why, though, had there been no such notation in the computer banks?

To set them down, as on a totally unexplored planet, was unlike any previous knowledge Kai had of EEC. Gaber's theory of planting the expedition returned to haunt his thoughts. EV had waited for their all-safe-down and conveniently disappeared in search of that storm. But there were the youngsters, more of an afterthought as members of the expedition than planned personnel. Above all else was the urgent need of the transuranics. Between the kids and the energy, Kai was certain he could discount Gaber's gloomy presentiment.

Even with the ability to pinpoint the exact location of the faintly signalling core, it took Gaber and Kai some hard slogging through dense and dangerous sword plants and some heavy digging to pull it from its site.

'Why, why, it looks like the ones we have,' said Gaber in a surprise that was almost outraged.

'No,' said Kai, turning the device thoughtfully in his hand, 'the case is fatter, the crystal dimmer and it feels old.'

'How can a core feel old? Why the casing isn't so much as scratched, or dull!'

'Heft it yourself. It feels old,' said Kai with a touch of impatience and he was somewhat amused to see Gaber hesitantly examine the old core, and quickly hand it back.

'The Theks manufacture them, don't they?' the cartographer said, giving Kai a sideways look.

'They have done but I think . . . Gaber, it won't wash.'

'But don't you see, Kai? The Theks know this planet has been surveyed. They're back for some reason of their own. You know how they like to watchdog a likely colony . . .'

'Gaber!' Kai wanted to shake the older man, shake him out of his asinine and dangerous notion that the expedition had been planted. But, as he stared at the man's eager, intense face, Kai realized how pathetic the cartographer was. Gaber must surely know this would be his last mission and was vainly hoping to extend it. 'Gaber!' Kai gave the man a little shake, smiling kindly. 'Now, I do appreciate your confiding your theory to me. You've done just as you should. And I appreciate the facts on which you base the notion but please don't go telling anyone else. I'd hate giving the heavy-worlders any excuse to ridicule one of my team.'

'Ridicule?' Gaber was startled and indignant.

'I'm afraid so, Gaber. The purpose of this expedition was too clearly set out in the original programme. This is just an ordinary energy-resource expedition, with a bit of xenobiology thrown in as practice for Varian, and to keep the heavy-worlders fit and the youngsters occupied while the EV chases that cosmic storm. Just to reassure you, though, I'll query EV about your theory in my next report. If, by any remote chance, you're correct, they'd tell us. Now we're down. In the meantime, I really do advise you to keep your notion between us, huh, Gaber? I value you as our cartographer too highly to want you mocked by the heavy-worlders.'

'Mocked?'

'They do like their little jokes on us light gravs. I don't want them to have one on you. We've a laugh for them, all right – on the Theks – with this,' and Kai held up the core. 'Our rocky friends are not so infallible after all. Not that I blame them for forgetting all about this planet, considering how it smells.'

'The heavy-worlders would make me a joke?' Gaber was having difficulty in accepting the possibility but Kai was certain he'd found the proper deterrant to keep the man from spreading that insidious rumour.

'Under the present circumstances, yes, if you came out with that notion. As I mentioned, we have the youngsters with us. You don't really think the Third Officer of EV is planting her son?'

'No, no, she wouldn't do that.' Gaber's expression changed from distressed to irritated. 'You're right. She'd've opposed it.' Gaber straightened his shoulders. 'You've eased my mind, Kai. I hadn't really *liked* the idea of being planted: I've left research unfinished and I only accepted this assignment to try and get a fresh perspective on it . . .'

'Good man.' Kai clapped the cartographer on the shoulder and turned him back towards the sled.

It occurred to Kai that he'd have all the arguments to press again once Gaber, and the others, learned that the EV had not picked up the secondary reports. He'd worry about that when the time came. Right now he had more to ponder in the ancient core in his hand. He didn't think they had any apparatus for dating the device in the shuttle. He couldn't remember if it had ever come up in discussion how long one of these cores could function. Portegin was the man to ask. And wouldn't he be amazed at what his malfunctioning screen was recording?

In fact, Portegin was already puzzling over the print-out when Kai and Gaber strode into the chart dome.

'Kai, we've got some crazy echoes on the seismic . . . what's this?'

'One of those echoes.'

Portegin, his lean face settling into lines of dismay, weighed the device in his hand, peered at it, turning it round and round, end for end before he looked with intense accusation at Kai.

'Where'd you get this?'

'Approximately here,' said Kai, pointing to the gap in the line of old echoes on the screen.

'We haven't cored that area yet, boss.'

'I know.'

'But, boss, this is Thek manufacture. I'd swear it.'

Margit, who'd been filling in her report, came over to the two men. She took the core from Portegin's unresisting hand.

'It feels heavier. And this crystal looks almost dead.' She regarded Kai for an explanation.

He shrugged. 'Gaber saw the echoes on the recorder, thought you'd mucked it up, Portegin . . .' he grinned as the mechanic growled at the cartographer. 'But I decided we'd better check. This was what we found.'

Margit made a guttural noise, deep in her throat, of disgust and irritation. 'You mean, we've spent hours doing what has been *done*! You wit-heads could have saved us time and useless energy by rigging that screen right off.'

'According to our computer banks, this planet had never been surveyed,' Kai said in a soothing drawl.

'Well, it has been.' Margit glowered at the screen. 'And you know, we've paralleled their line almost perfectly. Not

41

bad for a first working expedition, is it,' she added, talking herself into a better frame of mind. 'Hey,' she said in a much louder, less happy tone of voice, 'no wonder we couldn't find anything worth the looking. It'd been got already. How far does the old survey coring go?'

'Stops at the edge of the shield, my dear girl,' said Portegin, 'and now that we know from the old cores where the shield ends, we can start hitting some pay-dirt for a change. I don't think we've done too much duplication – except in the north and north-east.'

Kai thanked the compassionate computer who had put those two on this team with him: they might complain a bit, but they'd already talked themselves into a positive frame over the duplicated effort.

'I feel a lot better now, knowing there was a good reason we couldn't find any pay-dirt at all!' Margit studied the screen and then pointed at several areas. There's nothing here, and here. Should be!'

'Signals are very faint,' Portegin said. 'Some may have just give up the ghost. If everything else there is worked out, is there any point in setting new cores, Kai?'

'None.'

Aulia and Dimenon entered the cartography dome, closely followed by the other four geologists.

'Guess what Kai and Gaber found?' asked Margit. 'They found out why we couldn't find anything . . . yet!'

Expressions of surprise and displeasure greeted this statement. So Kai and Gaber repeated their afternoon's activities and the relief that spread throughout the room was reassuring to the team leader. Everyone had a turn at examining the old device, comparing it with those they were setting, joking about ghosts and echoes.

'We can set up secondary camps right on the edges of the shield,' Triv was saying excitedly. 'Can we start tomorrow, Kai?'

'Surely, I'll reassign everyone to more profitable areas, hopefully. Let me work it out. And Bakkun, I'll be out with you tomorrow.'

The meal gong sounded, reverberating under the force-screen so he dismissed them all, staying behind briefly to re-schedule flights for the morrow. They would have to set up secondary camps, as Triv suggested, but Kai wasn't all that keen to dissipate their complement. Varian hadn't yet had a chance to catalogue the worst of the predators and, despite the personal force-screens, a team could be caught too far away for timely help to arrive. That predator he'd seen today wouldn't be stopped by a puny personal force-screen. He also couldn't hold the teams back from discovering deposits: they got credit bonuses based on the assays of their indivi-dual discoveries. That was one reason why the lack of finds so far had had a serious effect on their morale. He couldn't risk a further check to their spirits and ambitions. He also couldn't risk sending them out against predators like those he'd seen today. He must have a chat with Varian.

He emerged into an insect-noisy night. The force-screen, arcing over the encampment, was aglow with blue spits of light as nocturnal creatures tried to reach the tantalizing floodlights which illuminated the compound.

Had that other survey party, millenniums ago, camped here? Would another group, millenniums hence, return when his cores emitted shallow ghost blips on another screen?

Were they really planted? The disturbing thought bobbed to the surface of his reflections, much as the aquatic monsters had been triggered by the shadow of the sled over the water. He tried to push down the notion. Had one of the others been tipped off privily? Varian? No, as co-leader, she was the least likely to have been informed. Tanegli? And was that why he was so willing to search out edible fruits? No, Tanegli was a sound man, but not the sort to be given private instructions while the team leaders were keyed out.

Not quite reassured within his own mind, Kai decided that congenial company would disrupt the uneasy tenor of his thoughts and he strode more purposefully towards the largest dome and his meal.

CHAPTER THREE

Varian was diverted by Kai's reception of the fruit when it was served as the evening meal. Divisti and Lungie had collaborated and the table was spread with the fruit in its natural form, sliced into green juicy portions: fruit synthesized as a paste, reinforced with nutrients and vitamins; fruit added to the subsistence proteins; stewed fruit, dried fruit. Kai fastidiously tasted a minute piece of the fresh sliced, smiled, made polite noises and finished his meal with the paste. Then he complained of a metallic aftertaste.

'That's the additives. There's no aftertaste with the fresh fruit,' Varian told him suppressing a mixture of annoyance at his conservative tastes and amusement at his reaction. The ship-bred were wary of anything in its natural form.

'Why cultivate a taste for something I can't indulge?' Kai asked when she tried to get him to eat more of the fresh fruit.

'Why not indulge yourself a little, while you have the chance? Besides,' she added, 'once you have the taste, you can programme it into any synthesizer, and duplicate it on shipboard to your heart's content.'

'A point.'

Varian had decided some time ago that it was just these little ship evolved differences that fascinated her about Kai. He wasn't physically that much different from the attractive young men she'd known on the various planets of her childhood and early specialist's training. If anything, Kai kept himself more physical fit in the EV's various humanoid sports facilities than his planet-based contemporaries. He'd a lean, wiry frame, slightly taller than average, taller than herself and she was not rated short on any normal Earth-type planet being 1.75 metres tall. More important to her in Kai than mere handsomeness which he had, was the strength in his face, the sparkle of humour in his brown eyes and the inner serenity that had commended him when they'd met in the

EV's humanoid dining area. She'd quickly recognized the aura of Discipline about him and been overwhelmingly relieved that he was a Disciple, and amused that his having passed the Training mattered to her on such short acquaintance. She'd accepted Discipline not that long ago herself, however much it meant that she could continue to advance in FSP service. A leader had to have Discipline since it was the only personal defence against other humanoids permitted by FSP and EEC, and of inestimable value in emergency situations.

Varian had been quite willing to develop a relationship with Kai and had privately done a good bit of private crowing when she'd unexpectedly been tapped as a xenob on his geology expedition to Ireta.

'And what's this I hear? This planet's been raped before?'

'The shield land mass we're on has certainly been stripped,' Kai replied, grinning a little at her blunt phrase. 'Portegin only got the seismic screen rigged last night. Gaber thought it was malfunctioning because we got echoes where we'd cored, and faint impulses where we hadn't. So I did a decco and found an old old core.'

Varian had already heard many of the details. 'We were informed during our briefing on shipboard that the system had been in storage a long time.'

'Well, there was no mention made of a previous geological survey.'

'True,' and Varian looked at a vague middle distance thoughtfully as she drawled out the affirmative. There had been sort of a last minute rush to assemble this Iretan expedition, though the Theks and Ryxi had been scheduled for their respective planets for some months. 'My team was sure added in a hurry. After they got print-out of life forms from the probe scan.'

'With all due respects, co-leader, the inclusion of your team doesn't puzzle me as much as no mention of a previous coring.'

'I quite appreciate that. How old d'you think the cores are?'

45

'Too scorching old for my liking, Varian. The line end with the stable shield area!'

Varian drew breath in a whistle. 'Kai, that would mean millions of years. Could even a Thek manufactured device last *that* long?'

'Who knows? C'mon, you can have a look at the device yourself. And I've some tapes to play for you that I think you'll like.'

'Those flying things Gaber was raving about?'

'Among others.'

'Sure you won't have one more piece of fresh fruit?' She couldn't resist teasing him.

Kai gave her a fleetingly irritated look, then grinned. He had an engaging smile, she thought, and not for the first time. They'd seen a good deal of each other in the planning stages but far too little now they had to deal with their separate responsibilities.

'I've had a sufficiency to eat, thank you, Varian.'

'And I'm a glutton, huh?' But she snatched up one more slice from the platter. 'What are these avians like? I don't trust Gaber's observations.'

'They're golden furred and I'd hazard that they're intelligent. Curiosity occurs only with intelligence, doesn't it?'

'Generally, yes. Intelligent fliers? Raking ramjets, this'll throw the Ryxi into loops.' Varian crowed with delight. 'Where'd you encounter them?'

'I went to see those coloured lakes of Berru's, and startled them out of the cliffs. By the way, the lakes harbour monsters every bit as big and dangerous as those swamp dwellers we saw this morning.'

'This planet goes in for big things . . .'

'Big puzzles, too.' They had entered the cartography dome now and Kai picked up the old core and handed it to her. 'Here's my latest.'

Varian hefted it in the palm of one hand. She saw another core on the table. 'Is this one of yours?'

Kai looked up from the tape cannisters he was sorting through and nodded.

Side by side, she could see the slight differences in circumference, length and weight.

'Does this previous coring explain why you've had so little luck in finding any cores?'

'Yes. The shield land has been stripped. My gang was relieved to know there was a good reason – this planet ought to be full of pay dirt. Now, however, we'll have to set up secondary camps in the new fold mountains . . .'

'Secondary camps? Kai, that isn't safe. Even if the worst you'd have to contend with is fang-face . . .'

'Fang-face?'

'Well, that's what I call whatever chewed a piece off Mabel's flank.'

'Mabel?'

'Must you keep repeating me? I find it a lot easier to name 'em than keep calling 'em "herbivore number one" or "predator with teeth A".'

'I didn't know you'd seen the predator?'

'I haven't. I can postulate from his tooth marks . . .'

'Would this be fang-face?' asked Kai as the tapes he and Gaber had made that afternoon began to appear on the viewing screen. He punched a hold on the one shot they'd had of the predator's head.

Varian let out a squeak as she got a good look at the toothy, snarling head, the angry little eyes upturned to the sled as the creature had flashed across the small clearing.

'Yes, that could be the villain. Six metres in the shoulder, too. You couldn't set up secondary camps that would keep him out. He could flatten you even with a couple of force-screen belts on you. No, I wouldn't advise secondary camps until we find out how far these sweethearts range.'

'We could move the shuttle . . .'

'Not until Trizein has completed his current run of experiments. And why move? Are we low on power for travel?'

'No, but I was considering the commutation time. Cuts down effective time in the field.'

'True. Frankly, Kai, I'd prefer to scout an area before you set up a secondary camp. Even those herbivores like Mabel, useless as they are, could be dangerous stampeding from a fang-face. However,' she added, seeing he was adamant, 'every animal in creation is afraid of something. I'll figure out what animals you'd have to contend with in an area and we can set up some safe-guards around say, one larger, suitably situated secondary camp and your field teams would be relatively safe . . .'

'You don't sound certain.'

'I'm not certain about anything on this crazy planet, Kai. And your discovery today only makes my uncertainty more . . .' she grinned, 'certain!'

He laughed.

She took one more long appraising look at the predator's rows of needle sharp teeth and then asked Kai to roll the tape. 'Sure glad you were aloft when you met that fellow. Gaber managed to tag him? That'll help estimate his territorial sway. Oh, I say, aren't they lovely!'

The golden fliers were on the screen, and while it might have been the juxtaposition to the preceding predator, they seemed so benign and graceful.

'Oh, hold that frame, Kai, please!' Varian gestured for him to go back on the tape until she had the frame of the creature, suspended in its flight, its crested head slightly turned towards the camera so that both golden-coloured eyes were visible.

'Yes, I'd agree that it's intelligent. Is that a pouch under its beak for storing fish? And it's a glider, I think. Roll it, Kai, I want to see if that wing can rotate. Yes, see, there! As it veers away. Yes, yes. Much more advanced than that carrion eater this morning. Why is so much of our reaction dependant on the eye of a creature?' She looked up at Kai whose grey eyes widened with surprise.

'Eye?'

'Yes. The eyes of that little mammal today . . . I couldn't have left it behind, Kai, short of mutiny, once I'd seen the frightened lost confusion in its eyes. Much less the entreaty in Bonnard's and Cleiti's. Those swamp horrors, they had tiny eyes, in comparison to their skull shape . . . wicked, beady, hungry eyes.' Varian shuddered in recall. 'And that new predator's eyes . . . fang-face has a wicked appetite. Of course, it isn't a hard and fast rule – the Galormis were a hideous example of camouflaged intent . . .'

'You were on that expedition?'

Varian made a face. 'Yes, I was a very junior member on the team at Aldebaran 4 when they were encountered. My first assignment out of xeno-veterinary college. They had soft eyes, mind you,' which occasionally still haunted her sleep, 'mild-looking creatures too, softish, perfectly amenable until full dark – then – whammie!'

'Nocturnal feeders—'

'Bleeders! Sucked the blood and then chewed the flesh . . . like what's been feeding on Mabel . . . No, it couldn't be Galormis. Teeth are too big.'

'Why on earth call it Mabel?'

'Knew someone like her once, a walking appetite, hating the world around her, suspicious and constantly confused. Not much intelligence.'

'What would you name the avian?'

'I don't know,' she said after regarding the furry face. 'It isn't easy until you've actually met the creature. But this species has intelligence and personality. I want to see more of them!'

'Thought you would. Although we couldn't tag them. They moved too fast. Kept up with the sled at cruising speed.'

'Very good.' A yawn caught her unawares. 'All this fresh air, chasing wounded animals to doctor them what don't wish to be helped.' She stroked his cheek and gave him a regretful smile of apology. 'I'm going to bed. And you ought to, too, co-leader. Sleep on our puzzles. Maybe sleep'll solve 'em.'

Kai could have wished it had, but he woke the next morning feeling refreshed and the teams, when assembled, were in such good spirits that his rose, too.

'I've discussed secondary camps with Varian. Until she has catalogued the habits of the predators, she can't guarantee our safety,' said Kai, 'but she's going to set and search areas into which we can move, if we adhere to the safeguards she devises. Okay? Sorry, but you'll understand better if you've seen the marks on the herbivore's flank.' He noticed by the grim expressions that everyone had looked at the creature.

'Boss, what about the gaps in the old cores, here, here and here?' asked Triv, pointing out the areas south-west and due south.

'Faults,' said Gaber, slipping a scale transparency over the seismic map. 'I read a massive overthrust here. Good area to search now but any seismimic would have been crushed. Or subsided too far below the surface to transmit.'

'Triv, you and Margit explore that overthrust today. Aulia and Dimenon, your sector is here,' and he gave them the co-ordinates in the south-west, and to Berru and Portegin, explaining that he and Bakkun would try to explore the Rift Valley since there were old cores leading up to it. He stressed that they maintain safety procedures, tag or telltale animals when possible, and note and report any scavengers circling over what could be injured livestock specimens for Varian.

As Kai and Bakkun lifted in their sled, Kai saw Varian on her way down to the corral. He saw the herbivore, Mabel, busily eating her way through what trees remained in the enclosure.

Bakkun, who preferred to pilot, brought the sled on its south-east heading.

'Why didn't our Theks know this planet'd been cored?' the heavy-worlder asked.

'I haven't asked our Theks if they know. But Ireta was not marked as surveyed.'

'Theks have their reasons.'

'Such as?'

'I do not presume to guess,' replied Bakkun, 'but they always have good reasons.'

Kai liked Bakkun as a team mate: he was inexhaustible, cool-headed like all his race, thorough and dependable. But he had no imagination, no flexibility and once convinced of anything, refused to change his opinion in the face of the most telling facts. Theks were, to him as to many of the short-spanned species, infallible and godlike. Kai did not wish, however, to enter into any argument with Bakkun, particularly on such a heresy as Thek fallibility proven in the existence of seismic cores on this planet.

Fortunately the telltale bleeped. Bakkun automatically corrected course and Kai watched the remote-distance screen attentively. This time it was more herbivores, running away from the sled's whine, through the thick rain forest, occasionally careering off trees so hard the top branches shuddered wildly.

'Come round again, Bakkun,' Kai asked and flipped up the tape switch, hanging in against his seat strap as Bakkun acted promptly to his order. He swore under his breath because none of the creatures crossed any of the clearings, almost as if they expected an aerial attack and were crowding under whatever cover they could find.

'Never mind, Bakkun. Continue on course. I thought I saw another flank-damaged beast.'

'We see them daily, Kai.'

'Why didn't you mention it in your reports?'

'Didn't know it was important, Kai. Too much else to mention bearing on *our* job . . .'

'This is a joint effort . . .'

'Agreed, but I must know how to contribute. I didn't know the mere ecological balances were essential knowledge, too.'

'My omission. But you would do well to report any unusual occurrence.'

'It is my impression, Kai, that there is nothing usual about Ireta. I have been a geologist for many standard years now and I have never encountered a planet constantly in a Mesozoic age and unlikely to evolve beyond that stage.' Bakkun gave Kai a sideways glance, sly and mysterious. 'Who would expect to find old cores registering on such a planet?'

'Expect the unexpected! That's the unofficial motto of our profession, isn't it?'

The sun, having briefly appeared in the early morning to oversee the beginnings of day, now retired behind clouds. A local ground fog made flying momentarily difficult so conversation was discontinued. Kai busied himself with the seismic overlay, checking the old cores which faintly glowed on the screen in response to his signal.

The cores advanced beyond the line of flight, right down into the rift valley, subsiding with the floor which composed the wide plateau. They were entering the valley now and Bakkun needed all his attention on his flying as the thermals caught the light sled and bounced it around. Once past the line of ancient volcanoes, their plugged peaks gaunt fingers to the now lowering rainclouds, their slopes supporting marginal vegetation, Bakkun guided the sled towards the central rift valley. The face of the fault block exposed the various strata of the uplift that had formed the valley. As the little sled zipped past, saucily irreverent of the frozen geohistory, Kai was filled with a mixture of awe and amusement: awe of the great forces still working which had formed the rift and might very well reform it times imaginable in the existence of this planet; and amusement that Man dared to pinpoint one tiny moment of those inexorable courses and attempt to put his mark upon it.

'Scavengers, Kai,' said Bakkun, breaking in on his thoughts. Bakkun gestured slightly starboard by the bow. Kai sighted the display on the scope.

'It's the golden fliers, not scavengers.'

'There is a difference?'

'Indeed there is, but what are they doing a couple of hundred kilometres from the nearest large water?'

'Are they dangerous?' asked Bakkun, with a show of interest.

'I don't think so. They are intelligent, showed curiosity in us yesterday, but what are they doing so far inland?'

'We shall soon know. We're closing fast.'

Kai slanted the scope to take in the groups on the ground. The fliers were now alerted to the presence of an unfamiliar aerial object and all the heads were turned upward. Kai saw threads of coarse grass hanging from several beaks. And, sure enough, as the sled circled, their elongated heads curiously followed its course. Some of the smaller fliers pecked again at the grass.

'Why would they have to come so far? For a grass?'

'I am not xeno-biologically trained,' said Bakkun in his stolid fashion. Then his voice took on a note of such unusual urgency that Kai swung round, scope and all and instinctively recoiled against the seatback. 'Look!'

'What the . . ,'

The rift valley narrowed slightly where a horst protruded and, from the narrow defile, emerged one of the largest creatures that Kai had ever seen, its stalky, awkward gait frightening in its inexorable progress. Sharpening the scope for the increased distance, Kai watched as the colossus strutted on its huge hindlegs into the peaceful valley.

'Krim! That's one of those fang-faced predators.'

'Observe the fliers, Kai!'

Loathe to withdraw his wary observation of the menace, Kai glanced up towards the golden fliers. They had assumed a curiously defensive formation in the sky. Those still grounded now grazed, if that could be considered a proper description for the quick scooping jabs. Varian must be right about the bill pouches, Kai realized, for the fliers' beaks had an elongated appearance. They must be stuffing the grasses into the pouches.

'The predator has seen them! Those still on the ground cannot get airborne in time if he should charge.' Bakkun's hand closed on the grip of the laser unit.

'Wait! Look at him!'

The heavy predatory head was now pointed in the direction of the fliers, as if the beast had just noticed their presence. The head tilted up, evidently registering the formation of the golden fliers. The creature's front legs, ludicrously small in comparison to the huge thighs and the length of the leg bone, twitched. The thick, counterbalancing tail also lashed in reaction to the presence of the fliers. Almost greedily, Kai thought. The biped remained stationery for another long moment and then dropped awkwardly forward, and began scooping up the grasses with its ridiculous forepaws, cramming great wads, roots, earth and all, into its huge maw.

While the two geologists watched, the fliers began to run

along what Kai now distinguished as a low bluff. They dipped almost to the grasses below before becoming safely airborne.

'They are trailing more grass, Kai.'

The leader focused the scope and saw the streamers trailing from hind and wing tip claws as the fliers beat steadily upward and away from the valley.

'Is that a seaward course they're on, Bakkun?'

'They are. And against a stiff head wind.'

Kai turned back to the browsing predator who hadn't paused in his voracious consumption of the grass.

'Now why would both fliers and that monster need the grass?'

'It does seem an unusual additive,' replied Bakkun, oblivious to the fact that Kai had been talking to himself.

'Would you set the sled down, Bakkun? At the other end of the valley from that beast. I want to get some samples of grass.'

'For Varian? Or Divisti?'

'Maybe for both. Strange that the predator didn't attempt to attack, isn't it?'

'Perhaps it does not like flier meat. Or they are formidable antagonists?'

'No. There was no hint of attack in the predator's manner, and only wary defence in the fliers. Almost as if . . . as if both recognized this as a place apart. That there was a truce here.'

'A truce? Between animals?' Bakkun sounded sceptical.

'That's what it looked like but the predator is certainly too primitive to operate on such a logical basis. I must ask Varian.'

'Yes, she would be the proper person to query,' said Bakkun, his composure restored, and he brought the sled to a smooth landing on the low bluff the fliers had used to take off.

'We are not golden fliers,' the heavy-worlder said in response to Kai's surprise at the landing spot. 'That creature may decide to season its grass with us.' He smoothly took over the scope. 'You collect. I will watch.'

The monster had not interrupted its feeding nor paid any attention to the sled. Kai dismounted with alacrity and, thumbing off his force-screen, began to gather grass. He was glad he had gloves because some of the blades had sharp edges, relatives to the sword plant, he decided. One clump came up, roots, earth and all, adding a new high to the malodourous air. Kai shook the earth free, remembering the birds had taken only the tops, not the root. Although the fliers had not gone in for the thicker bladed vegetation Kai took samples of everything in the vicinity. He stored his garnering in a container and resumed his place on the sled.

'He has not stopped eating grass, Kai,' said Bakkun, returning the scope to him.

As Bakkun eased the sled off the bluff and into the air, Kai kept the scope on the predator. It continued eating, not even lifting its head as the two geologists passed over it.

Bakkun, having been given no orders to the contrary, navigated the sled through the narrow end of the valley. Beyond, the ground fell away again, to a lower level without such luxuriant growth, the soil being sandier and supporting more of the tough shrub-type vegetation.

'The cores continue down this valley, Kai,' said Bakkun drawing his attention away from the monster and to the business at hand.

Kai looked at the seismic scanner. 'Last one just beyond that far ridge.'

'This rift valley is very old,' said Bakkun. Kai was pleased to hear the half-question in the man's voice. 'And the cores end beyond the ridge?'

'Indeed they do.'

'Oh!'

It was the first time Kai had ever heard uncertainty in a heavy-worlder's voice. He understood it and sympathized for he felt much the same way himself.

The overthrust above which they now passed had occurred at least a million years previous to their arrival on this planet. Yet the manufacture of the core unit was undeniably Thek. Unless, and the stray thought amused Kai, the Theks had copied an older civilization . . . the Others? The Theks as copyists restored Kai's sense of proportion. As he couldn't expect to compete with heavy-worlders on a physical basis, he ought not to compete with the Theks on a longevity performance. The here and now were important, too: twice, trebly important to him considering how short a span he could anticipate, even with all the miracles of medical science. He and his team had a job to do *now* on Ireta. Never mind that it had been done before when Man was still at the single cell stage swimming about at the beginning of a long evolutionary climb.

CHAPTER FOUR

With the help of Paskutti and Tardma, Varian managed to dress Mabel' flank wound. The beast had somehow managed to loosen the edges of the filmseal and, despite the force-screen over her corral, blood-suckers had attached themselves to the suppuration. She had opened the wound further in her frenzy to free herself from the ropes the heavy-worlders used to restrain her. They had to lash her head to her uninjured hind leg before Varian could approach her.

Fortunately, once she dislodged the blood-suckers, Varian thought the flesh looked healthy enough.

'I'm going to wash down and seal the entire leg,' she told Paskutti who was heaving with his exertions. 'Just as well I'm vetting the bitten instead of the biter. Hate to run into him.' She thought of the wicked head and the rows of vicious teeth glaring out of the frame Kai had taken.

'This creature couldn't put up much of a fight,' said Paskutti.

The edge to his tone surprised Varian into looking at him. She didn't expect to see any emotion registered on the heavy-worlder's blank features but there was an intensity in his pale eyes that gave her a momentary stab of fear. She got the distinct impression that the man was excited in some bizarre and revolting fashion, by the wound, by the concept of one animal eating another, alive. She turned back quickly to her task, loathe to let Paskutti know she'd observed him.

They completed the veterinary on Mabel without further struggle but her tail, when she was released from the ropes, lashed out so viciously that they all retreated hastily beyond range. Without the proximity of her well-wishers, Mabel seemed unable to continue her aggressive behaviour. She stopped mid-bellow and peered about her, as if puzzled by this unexpected respite. Her near-sighted eyes scanned so consistently above their heads that once they stood still,

Varian realized that Mabel would never see them. Mabel's worst enemy then, Varian decided, was much larger than the herbivore's considerable self, and generally perceived by smell to judge by the rapid dilation of Mabel's nostrils, and from a distance.

'What now, Varian?' asked Paskutti as they left the corral.

In his very lack of tone colour, Paskutti seemed to be impatient for her answer.

'Now, we check out what creatures inhabit the unknown land beyond the shield so that Kai and his teams can make secondary camps. We've the sled today, Paskutti, so if you'd get tapes, we can do some prospecting.'

'Weaponry?'

'The usual personnel defense. We're not hunting. We're observing.'

She spoke more harshly than she intended because there was an avid intensity about Paskutti's innocent question that was off-putting. Tardma was as blank as ever but then she never did anything, including smile, without glancing for permission from Paskutti.

As they re-entered the encampment for their equipment, Varian saw the children grouped about Dandy's enclosure, watching Lunzie feed it. Its thick little tail whisked this way and that either in greed or in enjoyment.

'Is Dandy eating well?'

'Second bottle,' said Bonnard with possessive pride.

'Lunzie says we can feed him when he gets to know us a bit better,' Cleiti added and Terilla nodded, her bright eyes big with such an incredible experience to anticipate.

Poor ship-bound wench, thought Varian whose childhood had been spent among the animals of many worlds with her veterinarian parents. She couldn't remember the time when she hadn't had animals to cuddle and care for. Small creatures brought to her parents for healing or observation had always been her particular charges once her parents had decided she was a responsible youngster. The only creatures she had never liked were the Galormis. Her instinct for animals had warned her the moment those soft devils had been discovered on

Aldebaran 4, but as a very junior xenob, she had had to keep her own counsel on her suspicions. At that she'd been lucky: she only had teeth marks on her arm where the Galormis which had attacked those in her dome had begun its nocturnal feeding. The creature had already killed its handler: its hollow incisors had proved to contain a paralytic with which it controlled its victims. Fortunately the night guard, alerted to trouble by the non-appearance of his relief, had roused the expedition, and the Galormis had been caught, contained and later exterminated. The planet was interdicted.

'We'll see how Dandy behaves himself first, Terilla,' said Varian, firmly believing in an old adage, "once bitten, twice shy". The originator had not had the Galormis in mind, but the application was apt.

'How's Mabel?' asked Lunzie, sparing Varian a glance.

Varian told her. 'We're scouting north today. Kai's teams will have to set up secondary camps soon but we don't want them encountering fang-faces, like the ones that ate Mabel. Also, the geology teams are supposed to report in if they sight any wounded beasts, so give us a toot right away, will you, Lunzie?'

The physician nodded again.

'Couldn't we come with you, Varian?' asked Bonnard. 'If you've the big sled? Please, Varian?'

'Not today.'

'You're on compound duty, and you know it, Bonnard,' said Lunzie. 'And lessons.'

Bonnard looked so rebellious that Varian gave him a poke in the arm, and told him to shape up. Cleiti, more sensitive to adult disapproval, nudged him in the ribs.

'We got out yesterday, Bon. We'll go again when it's proper.' Cleiti smiled up at Varian, though her expression was wistful.

A nice child, Cleiti, Varian thought as she and the heavy-worlders continued on to the storage shed for their equipment. Varian checked the big sled, despite the fact that Portegin had serviced it that morning.

They were airborne in good time, just after the morning's

first downpour. As seemed to be the rule on Ireta, the clouds then reluctantly parted, allowing the yellow-white sunlight to beat down. Varian's face-mask darkened in response to the change of light and she stopped squinting. Sometimes she found the curious yellow light of cloudy daytime more piercing than the full sun's rays.

They had to fly ten kilometres beyond the radius of the encampment before the telltale began to register life forms, most of them already tagged. The 'dead' perimeter had been expanding ever since they landed as if knowledge of the intruders had been slowly disseminating among the indigenous animals. This was a slow-cop world, Varian thought, for on more . . . civilized, was that the word she needed? Advanced, yes, that was more accurate. On more advanced worlds, the news of strangers seemed to waft on the outgoing wind of their descent, and inhabitants made themselves scarce . . . Unless, of course, it was an intelligent, non-violent world where everyone gathered around to see the new arrivals. Sometimes the welcome would be discreet, not defensive nor offensive, but distant. Varian thought of the defensive screen around the domes and snorted to herself. The thing wasn't needed – except to keep insects out. At least not under present circumstances, when the animals stayed far away. Maybe the solution to Kai's problem was simply to establish the physical secondary camp, complete with small force-screen, give the local wild-life a chance to drift away from the area, and then let his teams move in.

Yet there was fang-face! The size of him! She recalled tree tops shivering at his passage in the tape Kai had made. The main force-screen would burn him, probably dissuade him . . . there hadn't been much animal-life around those active volcanoes so creatures great and small on Ireta knew about fire and burn. The problem was the smaller screens weren't powerful enough to stop a determined attempt by fang-face if he were hungry, or scared, and that was what she had to allow for: the appetite of such predators as fang-face.

Varian had taped a course for the north-east, the vast high plateau, ringed by the tremendous mountains of the moon as

Gaber had called them. Two subcontinents had ground into each other, Gaber had told her pedantically, to force high those great stone peaks. The plateau beneath them had once been ocean bed. Anyone returning to that area had been enjoined by Gaber and Trizein to look for fossils on the rock faces. It was here, at the foot of the new fold mountains, that Kai hoped to start finding pay dirt. This was well beyond the ancient corings. For some reason, the discoverey of the old cores reassured Varian. Kai appeared worried about them and she couldn't imagine why. EEC wasn't likely to lose a planet they'd already twice explored. Besides, the Theks lived long enough to correct any mistakes they made – if they ever made any. Or maybe it was because they had time enough to correct any that it only appeared they were infallible.

Between the plateau they were heading for, with its coarse ground cover, not quite grass and not really shrub or thicket, was a wide band of rain forest through which Mabel's ilk passed, and where a fang-face was liable to lurk. Far to the east were clouds of volcanic activity, and occasional thunders, not meteorological in origin, rumbled to the sensors of the sled.

They spotted one set of circling scavengers and landed to investigate, but the creature had long since been reduced to a bony structure, any evidence of beast-gouging long gone. The dead weren't carrion long on Ireta. Tenacious insects were riddling the skeleton with industrious pinchers so that the bones would be gone in the next day. The tougher skull was intact and Varian, first spraying with antiseptic, examined it.

'One like Mabel?' asked Paskutti as Varian turned the skull from side to side with her boot.

'Crested at any rate. See, the nasal passage extends . . . I'd say Mabel and her kind smell a lot better than they see. Remember her performance this morning?'

'Everything smells on this planet,' replied Paskutti with enough vehemence to cause Varian to look up. She thought he was being humourous: he was deadly serious.

'Yes, the place stinks but if she's used it, she'd catch the

61

overlying odours and take appropriate action. Yes, it's her nose that's her first line of defence.'

She took some three dimension close-ups, and broke off, with some effort, a piece of the nasal cartilage and a sliver of bone, for later study. The skull was too cumbersome to transport.

The scavengers stayed aloft, but as soon as Varian lifted the sled they descended as if they hoped the intruders had discovered something they'd missed in the well-picked carcase.

'Waste not, want not,' Varian muttered under his breath. Life and death on Ireta moved swiftly. Small wonder that Mabel, grievously wounded though she was, had struggled to stay on her feet. Once down, the wounded seldom rose. Had she done Mabel any favours, succouring her so? Or had they merely postponed her early death? No, the wound was healing: the gouging teeth had not incapacitated muscle or broken bone. She'd live and, in time, be completely whole again.

The sled now approached the general grazing area where they'd found Mabel. Varian cut out the main engine, setting it to hover. The herd was there, all right. Varian caught sight of the mottled hides under broad and dripping tree leaves, down-wind of the creatures. They'd been too precipitous before and scared the herd off, with the exception of Mabel who hadn't been able to run fast enough.

Varian wondered at the intelligence level of the herbivores. You'd think this species would have learned to set out sentinels, the way animals on other inimicable worlds did, to forewarn the main herd of the arrival of dangerous predators. No, the size of the brain in that bare skull had been small, too small, Varian realized, to guide that great beast. A tail brain, perhaps? Long ago, far away, she'd heard of that combination. Not uncommon to have a secondary motor control unit in so large a beast. And then the nasal passages had pushed the brain case back. More smell than sense, that was Mabel!

'I see one, flank damaged,' said Tardma, peering over the port side. 'Recent attack!'

Varian sighted in on Tardma's beast and suppressed a shudder. She saw the bloodied mess of flank and wondered at the stoicism of the injured beast, chomping away at tree leaves. Hunger transcending pain, she thought. That's the dominant quest on this planet, the ease of hunger.

'There is another one. An older wound,' Paskutti said, touching Varian's shoulder to direct her attention.

The wound on the second beast was scabbed over, but when she intensified the magnification she could see the squirming life that was parasitic to the wound. Occasionally the herbivore interrupted its feeding to gnaw at its flank, and masses of the parasites were dropping off, their hold on the raw flesh loosened.

Slowly moving and staying down-wind of the herd, they made their survey. With few exceptions, the herbivores all displayed the gruesome flank gouges. And the exceptions were the young, the smaller specimens.

"They can run faster?' asked Tardma.

'Not juicy enough, more likely,' replied Varian.

'Protected by the adults?' asked Paskutti. 'You remember that the smallest ones ran in the centre of the herd when we first encountered this species.'

'I'd still like to know why . . .'

'We may find out now,' said Paskutti, pointing below.

At the furthest edge of the rain forest, one of the herbivores had stopped eating and had stretched itself up on its hindlegs, its crested head pointing steadily north. It dropped suddenly, wheeling, emitting a snorting kind of whistle as it began to run due south. Another beast, not alarmed by the departure of the first, seemed to catch the same scent. It too, whistled, dropped to all fours and began to trundle south. One by one, independently, the herbivores moved away, the smaller ones following the elders, and gradually overtaking them. The whistles grew more noisy, frightened.

'We wait?' asked Tardma, her blunt fingers twitching on the controls.

'Yes, we wait,' said Varian, uncomfortably aware of the suppressed eagerness in Tardma's manner.

They didn't have long to wait. They heard the crashing approach some seconds before seeing it, a pacing creature, head

63

low, short forepaws extended as it ran, its thick heavy tail counterbalancing the heavy body. The big jawed mouth was open, saliva foaming through but not obscuring the rows of spikey teeth. As it ran past the hovering sled, Varian saw its eyes, the hungry little eyes, the vicious eyes of the predator.

'Are we following?' asked Tardma, her voice curiously breathy.

'Yes.'

'To stop the ecological balance?' asked Puskutti.

'Balance? What that creature does is not balance, that's not killing for need: that's maiming for pleasure.'

Varian felt herself inwardly shaking with the force of her words. She ought not to get so upset.

'Perhaps, perhaps not,' said Paskutti and started the drive, to follow the predator.

Though it was not always in the scope, its course was easily followed by the broken or shaking trees, the sudden flurries of avian life forms or the startled scampering of small ground creatures. Its speed was considerably more than the lumbering herbivores and it was only a matter of time before it overcame the distance between them. If Varian found herself responding to the chase stimulus with quickened breath, dry throat and internal quivering, she was astounded by the metamorphosis of the heavy-worlders. For the first time since she had worked with them, they were displaying emotion: their faces contorted with an excitement, a lust, an avidity that had nothing to do with civilized reactions.

Varian was appalled and had she been at the controls instead of Paskutti, she would have veered away from the finale of this chase. That, in itself, would have been an act to undermine her authority over the heavy-worlders. They were tolerant of light gravity physical limitations, but they would have been contemptuous of moral cowardice. She had, after all, Varian realized, organized this expedition to discover how dangerous the predator was to the herbivores and to secondary camps. She couldn't turn aside becuse of squeamishness. And she didn't understand her own reactions. She'd seen more hideous forms of death, worse battles of animal against animal.

The predator had caught up with the main herd. It singled out one beast, pursuing the terrified animal into a cul-de-sac caused by fallen trees. Frantic, the herbivore tried to climb the trunks but it had ineffectual forefeet for such exercise and too much bulk for the logs to sustain. Bleating and whistling, it slid into its predator's grasp. With one mighty blow of a hindleg, the carnivore downed the fright-paralyzed herbivore. The predator measured a distance on the quivering flank; its front paws, far smaller than the massive hindlegs, were almost obscene in this gesture. The herbivore screamed as the predator's teeth sank into the flank and ripped off a hideous mouthful. Varian wanted to retch.

'Frighten that horror away, Paskutti. Kill it!'

'You can't rescue all the herbivores on this world by killing one predator,' said Paskutti, his eyes on the scene below, shining with what Varian recognized as a blood lust.

'I'm not rescuing all of them, just this one,' she cried, reaching for the controls.

Paskutti, his face once more settling into the more familiar, emotionless lines, switched the sled to full power and dove at the carnivore which was settling itself for a second rending bite. As the sled's exhaust singed its head skin, it roared. Rearing up, counterbalanced by the huge tail, it tried to grab at the sled.

'Again, Paskutti.'

'I know what I'm doing,' said Paskutti in a flat, dangerous voice.

Varian looked at Tardma, but she, too, had eyes for nothing but this curious battle. Why, thought Varian, appalled, he's playing with the predator!

This time Paskutti caught the predator off-balance. To keep upright, it had to release the herbivore.

'Get up, you silly creature. Get up and run,' cried Varian as the whistling, bleating grass-eater remained where it had fallen, blood oozing from the bitten flank.

'It hasn't wit enough to know it's free,' replied Tardma, her tone even but scornful.

'Drive the carnivore back, Paskutti.'

Varian needn't have spoken for that was what the heavy-worlder was doing. The predator, now recognizing an enemy above it, attempted to bat the menace from the sky with its forelegs and massive head. Instead, it was driven, back, back, away from the herbivore.

Paskutti played with the creature who impotently tried to defend itself. Before Varian realized what Paskutti intended, the man swung the sled and let a full blast of its jets into the predator's head. A bellow of pain assailed their ears as the sled accelerated violently forward, throwing Tardma and Varian against their straps. They were thrust in the other direction as Paskutti veered back to survey the effect of his chastisement.

The carnivore was trying to get its forepaws to its face, now blackened and bleeding from the jet blast. It rolled its head in agony as it lurched blindly about.

'Now let us see if it has learned a lesson,' Paskutti said and drove the sled back towards the beast.

It heard the sled, roared and stumbled wildly in the oppo-site direction.

'There, Varian. It has learned that a sled means pain. That one won't bother any area where it hears sleds.'

'That wasn't what I was trying to do, Paskutti.'

'You xenobs get soft-hearted. It's tough, that killer. It'll recover. You will want to tend the wounded herbivore?'

Controlling her sudden revulsion of Paskutti with a tre-mendous effort, Varian nodded and busied herself with her veterinary supplies. The herbivore was still on its side, too terrified to right itself and run. Its injured limb twitched and the exposed muscles rippled, each time causing the herbivore to whistle and bleat in pain. Varian ordered Paskutti to hover the sled directly over the creature which was oblivious to any-thing except its terror and pain. It was simpler to sprinkle over an antibiotic and spray the seal on from above. They continued to hover, at a higher altitude, until the beast realized that it was no longer in any danger and struggled to its feet. Then it sniffed about and, reassured, shook, bellowing as the reflex action caused discomfort in the leg. Abruptly it snatched at a hanging frond and munched. It looked for more food, turning about and then finally began to wander away from the trap, sniffing occasionally at the wind, bleating and whistling when it remembered it was wounded.

Varian felt Paskutti watching her. She didn't want to meet his eyes for fear he would see her revulsion of him.

'All right, let's extend our search in this area. We'll want to know what other life forms live in these foothills before the geologists can safely work here.'

Paskutti nodded and swung the sled towards the north-east again. They encountered and tagged three more herding types. Varian, still numbed by the earlier incident, gradually woke up to the fact that each of the new species must have had some common ancestor before evolutionary differences developed to put them into a sub-grouping.

When they returned to the base camp as the evening drenching began, Varian noticed that Tardma and Paskutti were as glad to be released from the close quarters of the sled as she was. She told Paskutti to check the sled over, Tardma to give Gaber the tape files and she went down to check on Mabel. The herbivore had reduced the trees of its enclosure to mere stumps. The full leg seal had held and Mabel did not appear to favour the injured leg. Varian was both eager and reluctant to release her patient but the logistics of supplying Mabel with sufficient fodder made her independence necessary. She decided to let Mabel go in the morning and follow it, at a discreet distance, in the sled. She would like to establish if it had any instinctive direction, if it had any communication with other members of its herd of species. Today the herbivores had responded to the dangerous approach of the predator on an individual basis. Too bad the silly fools couldn't gang up on their killer. By mass they could overpower it if they'd any courage at all. Or any leadership.

Could she stimulate Mabel's intelligence in any way, she wondered. And as quickly decided such a programme would be impossible. It would take too long and the chances of success with Mabel's brain space were unlikely. Mabel needed some physical modifications to achieve any measure of intelligence. There wasn't room enough in its skull for more than essential locomotion. Unless it had spare brains in its tail! And they'd be more motor control, too. Of course, she had encountered species with auxiliary nerve centres for controlling extremities while their intelligence, or main brain, was centrally located in the most protected part of their form. Man was, Varian reminded herself, not for the first time, rather badly designed. She understood the Theks held that opinion.

She was strolling thoughtfully back to the compound when she heard the whush of a returning sled and her name called. She caught sight of Kai's face. He looked happy about something. He was gesturing her to hurry up and join him. When she did, his usually composed face was brimming with excitement. Even Bakkun had an air of satisfaction about him.

'We've got some tapes you've got to see, Varian. We found one of your fang-faces . . .'

'Don't talk to me about *it*!'

'Huh? Had a rough day? Well, this will cheer you. I need your expert opinion.'

'I will take our finding up to Gaber,' said Bakkun, leaving the co-leaders together as he strode towards the cartographer's dome.

'You had a good day, then?' Varian put aside her negative mood. She had no right to depress Kai, or spoil his achievement.

'Very good. Just wait till you see,' he was guiding her towards the shuttle. 'Oh, how was yours? Could you clear that north-east section of foothills for a secondary camp?'

'Let's see your tapes first,' she said, and hurried him along to the pilot cabin.

'Admittedly, I don't know that much about animal behaviour,' he said as he slid the tape into the viewer and activated the playback, 'but this just doesn't seem logical. You see, we found the golden fliers a good hundred and sixty kilometres from the sea . . .'

'What? Doesn't make sense . . .'

The tape was playing now and she watched as the fliers came on the screen, the threads of grass visible in their beaks.

'You didn't think to . . .'

'I got samples of all the greens, grass and bush . . .'

'And they *are* green, instead of half-purple or blue . . .'

'Now watch . . .'

'Fardles! What's that thing doing there?' The predator had entered the valley, a dwarf figure until the close-up lens magnified it to a comparative life-size 'That's the beast that ate Mabel and . . .'

'Can't be the same one . . .'

'I realize that, but they are double-dangerous. We had one today, took a hunk out of another herbivore until we intervened. Why, scorch the raker, he's eating grass!' Astonishment silenced Varian. 'I wonder what's so essential in that grass. Damned curious. You'd think they'd have everything they need in their own environment. Now, he might be local. But the fliers couldn't be . . .'

'My thinking, too. Now this is the part that really baffles . . .'

The viewer now came to the scene in which fliers were aware of predator and it of them, the defensive line of the golden creatures and their orderly evacuation.

'Kai! Kai! Where are you, man?' They heard the voice of Dimenon, Kai's senior geologist. 'Kai!'

'Ho, Dimenon, we're up front,' Kai replied, pressing the hold on the viewer.

'We're here for the transuranics, aren't we?' asked Dimenon at his most dramatic as he burst into the small cabin, an equally excited Aulia beside him.

'You bet . . .'

'We found the mother's own end of a great whopping saddle of pitchblende . . . rich or I'll give you every credit in my account!'

'Where?'

'You know we were to follow the south-eastern track of the old cores, pick it up where it faltered? Well, where it faltered was at the edge of a geosyncline, the orogenesis is much later than this area. It was Aulia who noticed the vein, the brown lustre in the one sunny interval we had. We planted seismimics on a rough triangulation and this is the reading we got.' Dimenon brandished the print-out as one proferred a treasure. 'Rich – high up on the scale. Why, this one find alone justifies the entire expedition. And with all those new fold mountains, I'll bet this is the first of many. We struck it, Kai. We struck it!'

Kai was pummelling Dimenon and Varian was hugging Aulia with complete lack of inhibition while the rest of the geological team began to crowd into the compartment to add their congratulations.

'I was beginning to wonder about this planet. There were traces, yes, but there ought to have been more ore deposits . . .' Triv was saying.

'You forget, Triv,' Gaber said, inking smears on his face which was for once wreathed with genuine good humour, 'we're on old continental shield, not likely to have been much anyway.'

'All we had to do was get beyond the shield, and look what we've got already . . .' Dimenon again did his triumphant dance, waving the print-out tape like a streamer until it caught on Portegin's shoulder and began to tear. He ended his physical gyrations and carefully began to roll up the all-important tape which he stowed in his chest pocket. 'Over my heart forever!'

'I thought I was there,' Aulia teased him.

'This would seem to call for a celebration,' Lunzie said, putting her head round the door.

'Don't tell me you've got some joy juice hidden away somewhere?' cried Dimenon, waggling an accusatory finger at her.

'There's no end of ways to serve that fruit, you know,' she replied, her manner so blandly innocent that Varian whooped.

'Wouldn't you know Lunzie would come through?'

'Three cheers for Lunzie! The distilling dietician!'

'And how would you know it was distilled?' asked Lunzie suspiciously.

'Why else was Trizein rigging up a fractional distillation column?'

That warranted more laughter and congratulations which

was why Varian noticed the solemn heavy-worlders were absent. She said nothing about it, though she wondered. Surely Dimenon had made no secret of the find on his way up from the sled park. Where were the heavy-worlders that they wouldn't join in the expedition's first real triumph?

Lunzie was saying that she wasn't certain how good the brew would be. The product had had no time to settle or age but surely, Dimenon said in a wheedling tone, there'd be something to take the edge off the taste of it. The group began to file out of the shuttle, moving towards the general purpose dome. Varian saw no sign of the heavy-worlders but there was a light in the quarters they shared. Passing the central standard, she rang the alarm bell in alert sequence. The iris opening of the heavy-worlders' quarters widened slightly and massive shoulders and a head appeared, outlined by the light.

'Yes?' It was Paskutti.

'Didn't you hear, Paskutti? A massive find of pitchblende. Lunzie's distilled a beverage from the fruit. We're going to sample it by way of celebration.'

A huge hand waved and the iris closed.

'They being aloof again?' asked Kai, pausing in his progress to the large dome.

'They do have different enthusiams, it's true . . .' And abruptly Varian remembered the glimpse she'd had of Paskutti's intense reaction to the predator's attack on the herbivore.

'All work, no play . . . c'mon, Paskutti,' roared Kai. 'Tardma, Tanegli, Bakkun . . . you lot . . .'

The iris opened again and the heavy-worlders sedately crossed the compound to join the celebrants.

CHAPTER FIVE

By the time he had finished the first beaker of Lunzie's brew, Kai had considerably more respect for the versatility of the fruit and for Lunzie's resourcefulness which was already legend in the expedition. He might almost become a fruit-freak. His taste ran to a tart flavour in beverages and this had a jolt that was satisfying as well as to his liking.

He was startled to see Lunzie gravely pouring small beakers for the three youngsters but when he half-rose in protest, she gave him a placid nod. Kai watched as Bonnard sipped warily and then made a disappointed grimace.

'Aw, Lunzie, it's just juice.'

'Certainly. What else did you expect to get from me at your age?'

'You've added something, though, haven't you, Lunzie?' said Cleiti, smiling to make up for Bonnard's complaint.

'Yes, I have. See if you can determine what it is.'

'Probably something *good* for us,' said Bonnard in a mumble which Lunzie might not have heard for she was turning away.

Kai, thoroughly amused by the incident, moved to the dinner table and began to fill a plate. There was a mixture of synthesized and natural products, including a patty made of the algae Trizein had been cultivating. It tasted faintly of the hydro-telluride that permeated everything on this planet. Kai thought again that were it not for that stink, Ireta would be a wonderful assignment.

He stood a little apart as he ate, watching the other members of his teams, to gauge the general reaction to Dimenon's and Margit's find. A strike automatically increased the team's expeditionary earnings and there could be some resentment. Of course, now that they knew the shield lands were stripped, they'd go right into the nearest orogenic zones. Finds would be the rule, instead of the exception from now on.

And that would mean Kai would have to report the finds to EV. How long would he and Varian be able to suppress the fact that the expedition was no longer in contact with EEC? The teams would be expecting some sort of acknowledgement of their endeavours from the mother ship. Well, Kai thought, he was within standard procedural methods to wait until they'd done a thorough survey of the site and assayed the yield. That would give him a few days' grace. Then it was entirely within the realm of operations that EV might not strip the message from the beamer for another eight to ten days. After that, he and Varian might be forced to admit to the lack of communication. Of course, by that time, maybe the vessel would have passed beyond the interference of the storm and have picked up the backlog of reports. Kai decided not to worry about that problem right now. And took a good swig of Lunzie's brew. It did go down smoothly, with only the faintest trace of hydro-telluride.

Glancing around the room, Kai noticed that Varian was intently watching the heavy-worlders, her brows contracted in an expression of mild bewilderment. Paskutti was laughing, which was unusual enough, at something Tanegli had said. Could Lunzie's brew be having a loosening effect on the heavy-worlders? That shouldn't puzzle Varian. He went over to her.

'Never seen Paskutti laughing before?'

'Oh, you startled me, Kai.'

'Sorry, but they're . . . they're not drunk on the stuff, certainly . . .' She held her own beaker out, peering at it quizzically. 'They've had just as much as I have but they're . . . they're different.'

'I don't see any difference, Varian. Except this is only the second time I've ever seen Paskutti laugh and I've worked three standard years with the man. That's nothing to get upset about . . . or,' and he stared at her intently a moment, 'did something happen today?'

'Yes and no. Oh, just a rather brutal incident . . . a predator attacking one of Mabel's types. Nasty piece of work.' She gave herself a shake and then smiled with resolute good

73

humour at him. 'I'm too used to domesticated animals, I guess.'

'Like the Galormis?'

She shuddered. 'You do know how to cheer me up.' She stuck her tongue out at him and then laughed when he did. 'No, the Galormis were clever, in their own way. They had the wit to act appealing, like the beasts we have all come to know and love through the medium of the three-d tapes. My old practical vet instructor always warned us never to trust any animal, no matter how well we knew, liked or trusted it. But . . . oh, well. I have been with that dour bunch a lot, and I guess I'm imagining things. This is a happy occasion. So let's make it one. Tomorrow's going to be very busy. And,' she added, turning her body to shield her words from anyone nearby, 'what are we going to do about a message to EV?'

'Thought about that myself,' and Kai told her how he proposed they handle the problem.

'That's okay by me, Kai, and eminently sensible. Only I sure do hope we hear within that period. Say, you might ask the Theks in your next contact if they do remember anything about a previous expedition here.'

'Do I convey curiosity or disapproval because we were landed without any knowledge of a previous expedition?'

'Do the Theks appreciate either emotional prod?'

'I doubt it, but the trick is to get them actively thinking about anything.'

'By the time they've had their think, we could well be gone from here.' She paused and then, sort of surprised at her own words, added, 'You don't suppose that Elder Thek is from the original group?'

'Varian, it takes a million years to produce the tectonic changes that buried the other cores. Not even a Thek is that long-lived.'

'Its son, maybe? Direct memory transfer? I know they practise that between generations.'

'That could be it!'

'What?'

'How all knowledge of Ireta got lost. Inaccurate memory transfer.'

'There you go again, Kai, accusing the Theks of fallability. And here they've done half your work for you!'

Kai gave her a quick worried look but she was teasing him.

'Not the dangerous half . . . just sketched in the shields. Which reminds me, if you can spare them, I'd like to borrow the heavy-worlders tomorrow. We've got to move a lot of equipment and Dimenon says the terrain is wicked. Gaber will have to be on the spot for detailed mapping.'

'Who does that leave in camp on duty?'

'Lunzie prefers to stay in, on call. Divisti wants to do some tests and Trizein won't stir out of his lab. Oh, fardles, the younger contingent . . .'

'Don't worry about them. I'll take 'em. I'd like to see the pay dirt myself. It'd do them good. We can spin off and leave you to work in peace. I think Bonnard could manage the tell-tagger, even if you don't—'

'It's not that I don't, Varian . . .'

'I'm teasing you, Kai. But the kids'll be quite as useful for me to check the vicinity for the deposition of wildlife as the heavy-worlders. So long as we stay in the sled,' she added as she noticed Kai about to caution her.

Lunzie joined them at that point and Kai complimented her on the drink.

Lunzie frowned as she regarded the pitcher of liquid dubiously.

'It's not right yet. I shall distill it again, to see if I can't filter out that hint of hydro-telluride.'

'By all means keep at it, Lunzie,' said Kai and held out his beaker for her to fill, complaining when she did not.

'You don't need a big head for tomorrow. This fruit is potent.' Lunzie nodded towards the heavy-worlders whose deep laughs were rolling through the dome with increased frequency. 'They feel its effects and their metabolism can tolerate more alcohol than ours.'

'They do look drunk, don't they, Varian?'

'Drunk? Perhaps.' It could, Varian thought, account for the

way they were handling each other. Alcohol was a mild aphrodisiac for some species. She'd never heard that it affected the heavy-worlders that way. She was wondering if she ought to speak to them when suddenly, as if moved by a spontaneous signal, the heavy-worlders left the dome.

'It's good to see some who can recognize their limitations,' said Lunzie. 'I will take their tacit advice, and remove temptation.'

Varian protested that she'd only had one serving: Kai had had two. Lunzie gave her a splash more and then strode out of the dome. Gaber half-followed her, but a curt remark stopped him at the door. Scowling, the cartographer came back to Varian and Kai.

'The evening's only started,' he said in an aggrieved tone. 'Why did she have to remove the drink?'

'She's worried about its potency.' Varian studied the pale greenish liquid in her beaker with marked suspicion. 'It sure made an impression on the heavy-worlders.'

Gaber snorted. 'No need to deprive us because they have soft heads in spite of their heavy muscles.'

Kai and Varian exchanged glances because Gaber was slurring some of his words whether he was oblivious to the fact or not. He took a careful sip, closing his eyes to concentrate on an appreciation of the taste. 'First decent thing on this planet,' he said. 'Only thing that doesn't smell. And Lunzie makes off with it. Not fair. Just not fair.'

'We've a heavy day tomorrow, Gaber'

'Did *you* tell her to ration us?' Gaber was quite willing to transfer his irritation from Lunzie to Kai and Varian.

'No. She's the dietician and the physician, Gaber. This stuff is apparently not up to standard. There could be adverse reactions to it and tomorrow . . .'

'I know, I know,' and Gaber waved his hand irritably to cut off Kai's sentence. 'We've a big day tomorrow. Just as well we have something like this to sustain us when we're . . .' Now he abruptly concluded his sentence, glancing apprehensively at Kai who affected not to notice. 'It does have a funny taste to it.' He hurried off.

'Sustain us when . . . what, Kai?' asked Varian, concerned.

'Gaber came up with the ass-headed notion that we've been planted.'

'Planted?' Varian suppressed the words behind her hand and then let her laughter loose. 'I doubt it. Not on a planet as rich in the transuranics as this one. No way. Those ores are too badly needed. And it isn't as if they'd landed heavy equipment for us to do any sort of mining. Certainly not transuranic refining. Gaber's the original gloom guy. He can't ever look on the bright side of things.'

'I laughed at him, too, Varian, only . . .'

'Co-leader Kai,' Varian glowered at him sternly, 'of course you did. It's stupid, silly and I only wish that the other reports had been picked up from the satellite so I didn't have any doubts.' She gave Kai a frantic look, then shook her head. 'No, it won't wash. We're not planted. But, if we don't hear from EV, I wouldn't trust Gaber not to spread that rumour.' She looked at her empty beaker. 'Damn Lunzie! Just when I need a drop more.'

'I thought we'd decided not to worry about EV.'

'I'm not. Just grousing. I like that junk! It's got a certain curious jolt to it.'

'Probably a nutritional additive,' said Kai, remembering Bonnard's complaint.

Varian burst out laughing. 'Trust Lunzie for that. Our health is her first concern.'

Dimenon, his arm possessively about Margit, came strolling over to them. He couldn't have had more to drink than anyone else, since Lunzie had kept control of the pitcher, but his face was flushed and he was decidedly merry. He informed Kai that he insisted that the pitchblende mine be named after Margit. She was equally insistent that they share the triumph, as was customary, and the two fell to good-natured bickering, each calling for support from special friends in the team until everyone was involved in discussion.

Gaber was not the only one annoyed by Lunzie's precipitous departure with the drink, and Kai was surprised to hear a good deal of veiled complaints about the heavy-worlders. It caught him unawares as he'd been more sensitive to friction between the geological teams.

The next morning, he had additional cause for thought about the heavy-worlders for they were not operating in their usual stolid dependable fashion: they moved sluggishly, awkwardly, looked tired and were almost sullenly quiet.

'They couldn't have got hung over in two half-beakers,' Varian murmured to Kai as she, too, noticed the glum manner of her team. 'And their quarters were dark early. They ought to have got enough sleep.'

'If they got to sleep . . .' Kai replied grinning.

Varian dropped her jaw in surprise and then she giggled.

'I tend to forget they must have a sex drive. It's a weird cycle, compulsive in the rut, so to speak, on their own planet. Generally, they don't when they're on a mission.'

'There isn't a law against it for them, is there?'

'No, it's just they don't . . .' She seemed to find it mystifying. 'Well, they'll sweat it out on those slopes this morning,' she added, looking at the foothills that folded higher and higher until the overthrust mountains dominated the skyline. They were standing at the base of the saddle ridge of pitchblende, looking down the fold limb. The brown lustrous vein was visible where dirt had been blown clear. 'This is a fantastic deposit, Kai. And so is its location. Why one of the big mining ships can just squat right down and crunch up all of it without moving again.' She had emphasized her words by rolling her r's, and gesturing graphically with her fingers in claw-like attitudes.

'I didn't realize you'd worked with a geology team before.'

'Galorm was explored for its minerals, not its wildlife, Kai. Admittedly the wildlife made the beamlines but we xenobs were just along to catalogue another variation of Life.'

'Do you ever mind?'

'What? Being second?' She shrugged and smiled to reassure him. 'No, Kai. Energy is a lot more important than wildlife.'

'Life,' and he paused to stress the inclusiveness of the word, 'is far more important than any inanimate object . . .' he gestured to the pitchblende.

'Which just happens to be essential to sustain *life* – on other planets, and in space. We have to sustain, protect and investigate. I'm here to inspect the life that exists on Ireta, and you're here to insure that life elsewhere can continue on its grand and glorious scale. Don't fret on my account, Kai. The experience I gain here may just one day put me where I really want to be . . .'

'Which is . . .' Kai was also trying to see what Paskutti and Tardma were doing with a seismograph.

'Planetary preserver. Now,' she went on, noticing his diverted attention, 'I'd better enhance the reputation needed to be one by studying those fliers of yours. I can survey this area first.'

They both caught in their breaths as Tardma faltered, struggled to regain her balance and the backpack of delicate instrumentation which she was bringing up the far slope.

'What the fardles did Lunzie put in that joy juice of hers to queer them up so?'

'It's Ireta that's doing it to them! The drink didn't affect us that way. I'm off now, Kai. I've only to gather the youngsters.'

'I'll need the big sled back here, you know.'

'Yes, by sundown! Shout if you need it sooner,' she said, gesturing to her wrist comunit.

Bonnard was disappointed to be dragged away before the first seismic shot but, when Dimenon told him it would take several hours to set up, he went willingly with Varian.

Terilla had been enchanted by unusual flowering vines and, carefully wearing her thick gloves, had gathered different types which she had placed in the bags Divisti had given her for the purpose. Cleiti, who tended to be Bonnard's aide and assistant, regarded the younger girl's activity with supercilious disdain. Varian shooed them all towards the big sled and told them to settle in and belt up. She was checking the flight board when she was struck by the sled's elapsed hours of use. Surely she hadn't put twelve hours flight time on it yesterday? Even subtracting the two hours needed to reach these foothills, she couldn't have racked up more than six hours the day before. That left a huge whack unaccounted for – and made the sled due for a recharge and servicing.

She'd ask Kai about it when she returned. Maybe she simply hadn't recorded accurately, or the sled had been used here when she'd been busy elsewhere.

She showed Bonnard how to operate the tagger, Cleiti how to read the life-form telltale, and Terilla how to be sure the recorder was functioning as they'd be passing over relatively undetailed terrain. The youngsters were delighted to have some responsibility and listened attentively as Varian explained the quartering pattern she would follow as they surveyed the general vicinity for dangerous life forms. Although Varian was sceptical about the duration of their enthusiasm once the tasks had settled into routine, their exuberance made a nice change from the sober company of the heavy worlders.

The three young people hadn't had that much occasion to see the raw life of a virgin planet, and had had only the one trip since they'd landed on Ireta. They chattered happily as Varian lifted the sled and circled the geological site.

At first there wasn't much to telltale or tag. Most of the animal life was small and kept hidden from sight. Bonnard was jubilant when he tagged some tree-dwellers which Varian thought must be nocturnal since they didn't so much as move from their tree boles when the sled overpassed them. Terilla periodically reported the recorder functioning but the ground cover would make details of the area difficult to read. In the low foothills, as they quartered back towards the pitchblende saddle, the sled's noise flushed a group of fleet little animals which Bonnard gleefully tagged and Terilla triumphantly taped. Slightly put out by the success of the others, Cleiti's turn came when she read telltales of a cave-dwelling life form. They did not show themselves but the readings were low enough on the scale to suggest small creatures, burrowers or timid night beasts that would be unlikely to cause problems for any secondary camp.

In fact, Varian had to conclude that nothing of any potentially dangerous size could be found in the foothills surrounding the pitchblende discovery. Nonetheless, size did not, as she pointed out to the children, relate to the potential danger of a creature. Some of the smallest were the most deadly. The one you could hear coming was the safest: you could take evasive action. Bonnard snorted at the notion of running away.

'I like plants better than animals,' said Terilla.

'Plants can be just as dangerous,' replied Bonnard in a repressive tone.

'Like that sword plant?' asked Terilla with such innocence that Varian, who was suppressing her laughter at the girl's apt query, could not consider the child guilty of malice.

Bonnard growled at the reminder of his painful encounter with that particular plant and was patently trying to think of a put-down for Terilla.

'Your instruments are transmitting,' said Varian, to forestall a quarrel.

The sled was passing over an area of squat trees and thick undergrowth which triggered the telltale at a large enough scale and sufficient concentration to warrant some investigation. The terrain was rocky and steep which suggested the inhabitants were not ruminants. However, after circling without flushing the creatures, Varian decided that the area was far enough from the ore deposit to be a negligible danger. She marked the co-ordinates for later study when a group expedition could be mounted. Despite the general high level of violent life and death on Ireta, one could be too cautious. If Kai sited the secondary camp high enough up in the foothills to avoid the worst predatory life, the force-screen would be sufficient to deter poisonous insects and dangerous smaller animals. It wasn't as if a herd of Mabels was likely to come rampaging up the slopes and stampeding through the force-screen.

She finished her survey, cautioned the youngsters to check the seat belts they had loosened to attend to their instruments, and, tapping in the co-ordinates for the inland sea, gave the sled full power.

Even so it took a good hour and a half to reach their destination. She wished that Divisti had had a chance to run an analysis of the grasses which Kai and Bakkun had collected at the Rift Valley. The report might have given Varian some insight to the habits of the fliers but, perhaps it was wiser to observe these fascinating creatures without preconceived notions.

Varian was pleased with the behaviour of the youngsters on the flight: they asked more intelligent questions than she'd been led to expect from them, sometimes straying in areas of which she had little knowledge. They seemed annoyed that she was not a portable data reteival unit.

Cleiti was the first to spot the fliers, and preened herself for that feat later on. The creatures were not, as Varian had unconsciously expected, perched on the cliffs and rocks of their natural habitat, nor singly fishing. A large group – not a flock for that was a loose collection of a similar species, and the fliers gave the appearance of organization – was gathered above the broad end of the inland water, at its deepest part, where the cliffs narrowed to form the narrow isthmus through which the parent sea pushed the tide waters to flush the vast inland basin; a tide which seldom had force enough to crawl more than a few inches up the verge on the farthest shore, fifty kilometres away.

'I've never seen birds doing that,' Bonnard exclaimed.

'When did you ever see free birds in flight?' asked Varian, a bit chagrined that her tone emerged sharper than she'd intended.

'I have landed, you know,' said Bonnard with mild reproach. 'And there are such things as training tapes. I watch a lot of those. So, those aren't acting like any other species I've ever seen.'

'Qualifications accepted, Bonnard, I haven't either.'

The golden fliers were sweeping low in what had to be considered a planned formation. The sled was a bit too far for unaided vision of the observers to perceive exactly what happened to jerk the line of fliers to half their previous forward speed. Some of the fliers were dragged downward briefly but, as they beat their wings violently to compensate, they recovered their positions in the line and slowly, the whole mass began to lift up, away from the water's surface.

'Hey, they've got something in their claws,' said Bonnard who had appropriated the screen from Cleiti and had adjusted it to the distance factor. 'I'd swear it is a net. It is! And they're dragging fish from the water. Scorch it! And look what's happening below!'

Varian had had time to adjust her mask's magnification and the girls had crowded over the small viewer plate with Bonnard. They could all see clearly the roiling water, and the frenzied thrusts and jumps of the aquatic life which unsuccessfully tried to penetrate the nets and the captured prey.

'Nets! How in the raking rates do fliers achieve nets?' Varian's comment was more for herself than the children.

'I see claws half down their wings, there, where it goes triangular. Can't see clearly enough but, Varian, if they've an opposing digit, they could *make* nets.'

'They could and they must have, because we haven't seen anything else bright enough on Ireta to make 'em for 'em.'

Cleiti giggled, smothering the sound in her hand. 'The Ryxi won't like this.'

'Why not?' Bonnard demanded, regarding his friend with a frown. 'Intelligent avian life is very rare, my xenob says.'

'The Ryxi like being the only smart ones,' said Cleiti. 'You know how Vrl used to be . . .' Somehow the child lengthened her neck, hunched her shoulders forward, swept her hands and arms back like folded wings and assumed such a haughty expression by pulling her mouth and chin down that she exactly resembled the arrogant Vrl.

'Don't ever let him see that,' Varian said, tears of laughter in her eyes. 'But it's a terrific mime, Cleiti. Terrific.'

Cleiti grinned at their success as Bonnard and Terilla regarded her with expressions akin to awe.

'Who else can you do?' asked Bonnard.

Cleiti shrugged. 'Who did you want?'

'Not now, kids. Later. I want tape on this phenomenon.' The three youngsters immediately took their assigned

83

stations as the sled followed the burdened fliers towards the distant cliffs. Varian had time to dwell on the subtler implications of the fliers' fishing. The creatures were quite obviously the most intelligent species she had encountered on Ireta. Nor had she come across another cooperative avian race: at least, at this level. Bonnard's xenob was not accurate in saying that intelligent avian life was rare: *dominant* intelligent avian life was, however. So often winged life was in such desperate competition with ground based life for the same foods that all their energies had to be directed to the procurement of food, or the preservation of the home nest, and the succour of the young. When a life form specialized, dropping the forearm with manipulative skill for the wing of retreat, they lost a tremendous advantage in the battle of survival.

The golden fliers of Ireta seemed to have managed to retain the vestigial hand without expense to the wing, thus used their flight advantage beautifully.

Occasionally smaller fish fell from the nets, back into the sea, to cause more frothing as the submarine denizens struggled to secure the prizes. Twice, immense heads rolled avidly up from the deeps, futilely as the fliers passed with their tempting loads.

Now the four observers saw additional fliers materializing from the cloudy skies, swooping down to take positions along the edges of the nets, supporting the load and relieving the first fishers. Thus assisted, the formation picked up speed.

'How fast are they going now, Varian?' asked Bonnard for the xenob had been carefully matching the forward motion, staying behind but above the fliers.

'With this tail wind, I make it twenty kph, but I think they'll gain air speed with all this reinforcement.'

'They're so beautiful,' said Terilla softly. 'Even hard at work, they're graceful and see how they gleam.'

'They look as if they were travelling in their own personal sunlight,' said Cleiti, 'but there's no sun.'

'Yeah, what's with this crazy planet?' said Bonnard. 'It

stinks and there's never any sun. I did want to see a sun when I got a chance.'

'Well, here's your moment,' said Terilla, crowing with delight as the unpredictable happened and the clouds parted to a glimpse of the green sky and the white-hot yellow sun.

Varian laughed with the others and almost wished that the face-masks didn't adjust instantly for the change in light. The only way she knew that there was sun at the moment were the shadows on the sea.

'We're being followed!' Bonnard's amused tone held a note of awe.

Huge submarine bodies now launched up and slammed down on the shadow which the air sled cast on the waters behind it.

'I'm glad we're ahead of them,' Cleiti said in a small voice.

'There's the biggest crazy I've ever seen!' Bonnard sounded so startled that Varian turned round.

'What was it, Bonnard?'

'I couldn't tell you. I've never seen anything like it in all my born days, Varian.'

'Was the taper on it?'

'Not on *that*,' said Terilla, apologetically. 'Forward, on the fliers.'

'Here, let me have it, Ter. I know where to point.' Bonnard assumed control and Terilla moved aside.

'It's like a flat piece of fabric, Varian,' Bonnard was saying as he sighted across the stern of the sled. 'The edges flutter and then . . . it sort of turns over on itself! Here comes another!'

The girls gave small squeals of revulsion and delighted fear. Varian slewed round in the pilot seat and caught a glimpse of something grey-blue which did, as Bonnard said, flutter like a fabric caught in a strong breeze. She caught sight of two points half-way up one side (like claws?), then the creature flipped over, end for end, and entered the water with more of a swish than a splash, as Cleiti put it.

'How big would you say it was, Bonnard?'

'I'd judge about a metre on each side but it kept switching.

I've got good tapes of that last leap. I set the speed half again higher so you can play back for more detail.'

'That's using your head, Bonnard.'

'Here comes another! Rakers! Look at the speed on that thing!'

'I'd rather not,' said Terilla. 'How does it know we're here? I don't see any sort of eyes or antenna or anything. It can't see the shadows.'

'The fringes?' asked Bonnard. 'Sonar?'

'Not for leaping *out* of water,' replied Varian. 'We'll possibly find out how it perceives us when we can replay. Rather interesting. And were those claws I saw? Two of them?'

'That's bad?' Bonnard had caught the puzzled note in her voice.

'Not bad, Bonnard, but damned unusual. The fliers, the herbivores and the predators are pentadactyl which isn't an unlikely evolution, but two digits on a side flange?'

'I saw flying longies once,' said Cleiti in a bright helpful voice. 'They were a metre long and they undulated. No feet at all, but they could ripple along in the air for kilometres.'

'Light gravity planet?'

'Yes, Varian, and dry!'

The sun had slunk behind the clouds again and the thin noonday drizzle settled in so that the others laughed at her sour comment.

'Digits are important in evolution, aren't they, Varian?' asked Bonnard.

'Very. You can have intelligent life, like those avians, but until a species becomes a tool-user, they don't have much chance of rising above their environment.'

'The fliers have, haven't they?' asked Bonnard with a broad grin for his play on words.

'Yes, Bonnard, they have,' she replied with a laugh.

'I heard about them being in the rift valley, with grasses,' Bonnard went on. 'Is this why they got that type of grass? To make the nets?'

'There was a lot of thick tough grass around the place where

86

we saved Dandy, and that was a lot closer for them,' said Cleiti.

'You're right there, Cleiti. I've thought the fliers might need the rift valley grass for some dietary requirement.'

'I have some of the vegetation from the grove of fruit trees, Varian,' said Terilla.

'You do? That's great. We can do some real investigation. How clever of you, Terilla.'

'Not clever, you know me and plants,' said the girl, but her cheeks were flushed with reaction to the praise.

'I take back what I said about your stupid plants,' said Bonnard with unusual magnaminity.

'I'll be very keen to see how mature their young are,' Varian said, having quietly considered the curious habits of the golden creatures for a few minutes.

'How mature? Their young? Isn't that a contradiction?' asked Bonnard.

'Not really. You are born very young . . .'

Cleiti giggled. 'Everyone is, or you wouldn't *be* young . . .'

'I don't mean age, I mean ability, Cleiti. Now, let's see what comparisons I can draw for you ship-bred . . .'

'I lived my first four years on a planet,' said Terilla.

'Did you? Which one?'

'Arthos in the Aurigae section. I've touched down on two more and stayed for months.'

'And what animals did you see on Arthos?' Varian knew but Terilla so seldom volunteered any information, or had a chance to with such aggressive personalities as Cleiti and Bonnard.

'We had milk cows, and four-legged dogs, and horses. Then there were six-legged dogs, offoxes, cantileps and spurges.'

'Seen any tape on cows, dogs and horses, Cleiti? Bonnard?'

'Sure!'

'All right, cows and horses bear live young who are able to rise to their feet about a half hour after birth and, if necessary, run with their dams. They are therefore born mature and already programmed for certain instinctive actions and responses. You and I were born quite small and physically immature. We had to be taught by our parents or guardians how to eat, walk, run and talk, and take care of ourselves.'

'So?' Bonnard regarded Varian steadily, waiting for the point of her disgression.

'So, the horse and cow don't learn a lot from their parents: not much versatility or adaptability is required of them. Whereas human babies ...'

'Have to learn too much too soon too well and all the time,' said Cleiti with such an exaggerated sigh of resignation that Varian chuckled.

'And change half of what you learn when the info gets updated,' she added, sympathetically. 'The main advantage humans have is that they do learn, are flexible and can adapt. Adapt to some pretty weird conditions ...'

'Like the stink here,' put in Bonnard.

'So that's why I'm curious about the maturity of the fliers at birth.'

'They'd be oviparous, wouldn't they?' asked Bonnard.

'More than likely. I don't see that they'd be ovoviviparous ... too much weight for the mother if she had to carry her young for any length of time. No, I'd say they'd have to be oviparous, and then the eggs would hatch fledglings, unable to fly for quite some time. That might account, too, for the fishing. Easier to supply the hungry young if everyone cooperates.'

'Hey, look, Varian,' cried Bonnard who had not left off watching through the screen, 'there's a change-over on the net carriers. Bells! but they're organized. As neat a change-over as I've ever seen. I'll bet the fliers are the most intelligent species on Ireta.'

'Quite likely but don't jump to any conclusion. We've barely begun to explore this planet.'

'Are we going to have to go over all of it?' Bonnard was briefly dismayed.

'Oh, as much as we can while we're here,' she said in a casual tone. What if they had been planted? 'Apart from its odour, Ireta isn't too bad a place. I've been in a lot worse,'

'I don't really mind the smell . . .' Bonnard began, half in apology, half in self-defence.

'I don't even notice it anymore,' said Terilla.

'I do mind the rain . . .' Bonnard continued, ignoring Terilla's comment. 'And the gloom.'

At which point the sun emerged.

'Can you do that again whenever we feel the need of sunlight?' asked Varian as the girls giggled over the opportuneness.

'I sure wish I could!'

Once again the angle of the sun projected a distorted shadow of the sled on the water and the fish, large and small, shattered the surface in vain attempts to secure the reality of that shadow. Varian had Bonnard tape the attacks for later review. It was an easy way to catalogue the submarine life, she said.

'I sailed once on shore leave at Boston-Betelgeuse,' said Bonnard after the sun, and the predatory fish, had deserted them.

'You wouldn't catch me sailing on that!' said Cleiti, pointing to the water.

'I wouldn't, but something else would, wouldn't it?'

'Huh?'

'Catch you, silly face!'

'Oh, you're so funny!'

Additional fliers emerged from the clouds to relieve the net carriers who sped up and away, as if pleased to be free of their chore. The convoy, strengthened by the reinforcements, picked up speed, veering slightly east, towards the highest of the prominences. They were not, as Varian had assumed, going to have to cross the entire sea to reach a home base.

'Hey, that's where they're heading. I can see other fliers on the cliff top, and the front is all holey, with caves!' cried Bonnard, delighted.

'They live in caves to keep their furs dry, and their fledglings safe from the sea creatures,' said Terilla with unusual authority.

'Birds have feathers, stupid.'

'Not always,' Varian replied. 'And those fliers appear to have fur which is, sometimes, a variation of a feather, in some beasts.'

'Are we going to land and find out fur sure?' asked Bonnard in a ponderous tone of voice so everyone caught his pun. Cleiti swatted at him and Varian groaned, shaking her head.

'No, we're not landing now. It's dangerous to approach animals when they're feeding. We know where the fliers live now. That's enough for one day.'

'Couldn't we just hover? That won't disturb them.'

'Yes, we could.'

More of the golden creatures emerged from crevices and caves in the cliff, and gracefully swooped up to the summit which Varian could see was relatively flat for about five hundred metres where it dropped off into very rough and boulder-strewn slopes.

'What're they going to do now?' asked Bonnard. 'That net's too big to get in any one of those cave entrances . . . Oh . . .' Bonnard's question was answered as the entire group of fliers now carried the net up over the edge of the cliff and suddenly dropped one side, spilling the fish onto the summit plateau.

From every direction fliers converged on the catch. Some landed, wings slightly spread, to waddle in an ungainly fashion towards the shimmering piles of fish. Others swooped, filled their throat pouches and disappeared into their cliff holes. For all the varied approaches, the dispersal of the catch occasioned no squabbling over choice fish. As the four watched, there were periods when no fliers were picking over the fish. They did seem to be selective.

'Sharpen the focus on the viewer, Bonnard,' said Varian. 'Let's get some frames of what they didn't eat . . .'

'Those fringe things, the small ones.'

'Maybe that's why the fringe fliers were after us. They'd taken their young . . .' said Terilla.

'Nah!' Bonnard was contemptuous. 'The fringies hadn't

eyes, much less brains, so how could they be sentimental about their young?'

'I dunno. But we don't know that they aren't. Fish could have emotions. I read somewhere that . . .'

'Oh you!' Bonnard gestured her peremptorily to silence.

Varian turned, worrying that his attitude might bother the child since his tone was unwarranted but she seemed unperturbed. Varian promised herself a few choice words with Bonnard. And then vetoed the notion. The young of every species seemed to work things out among themselves fairly well.

She peered into the viewer herself, to see the rejects. 'Some aquatic creatures are capable of loyalties and kindness to their own species, but I'd say that the fringe organism is too primitive yet. They probably spawn millions of eggs in order for a few to survive to adulthood – to spawn again. Our fliers don't include them in their diet, though. Nor those spiny types. Bonnard, you've been helping Trizein and Divisti: take a good look! Seen any of those in the marine samples we've given them?'

'No. New ones on me.'

'Course, we sampled from the main oceans . . .' Most of the fliers had disappeared now and only the rejected specimens were left, to rot on the stone.

'Varian, look!' Bonnard, again at the screen, gestured urgently. 'I've got it lined up . . . look!'

Varian pushed his hand aside as he was so excited he was obscuring the view. One of the small fringers was moving, in that strange fashion, collapsing one side and flipping over. Then she saw what had excited Bonnard: unsupported by water, its natural element, the internal skeleton of the creature was outlined through its covering. She could plainly see the joints at each corner. It moved by a deformation of parallelograms. It moved once, twice more and then lay still, its fringes barely undulating, then not at all. How long had it survived without water, Varian wondered? Was it equipped with a dual set of lungs to have lived so long away from what was apparently its natural element? Was this creature on its way out of its aquatic phase, moving onto land?

'You got all that on tape, didn't you?' Varian asked Bonnard.

'Sure, the moment it started moving. Can it breathe oxygen?'

'I hope it can't,' said Cleiti. 'I wouldn't want to meet that wet sheet in a dark dripping forest.' She shuddered with her eyes tightly shut.

'Neither would I,' said Varian, and meant it.

'Couldn't it be friendly? If it wasn't hungry all the time?' asked Terilla.

'Wet, slimy, wrapping its fringes around you and choking you to death,' said Bonnard, making movements like his horrifying image.

'It couldn't wrap around me,' Terilla said, unmoved. 'It can't bend in the middle. Only on the edges.'

'It isn't moving at all now,' Bonnard said, sounding disappointed and sad.

'Speaking of moving,' said Varian glancing toward the one bright spot in the grey skies, 'that sun is going down.'

'How can you tell?' asked Bonnard sarcastically.

'I'm looking at the chrono.'

Cleiti and Terilla giggled.

'Couldn't we land and see the fliers up close?' asked Bonnard, now wistful.

'Rule number one, never bother animals when feeding. Rule number two, never approach strange animals without first closely observing their habits. Just because the fliers haven't attempted to take bites out of us doesn't mean they aren't as dangerous as those mindless predators.'

'Aren't we ever going to observe them up close?' Bonnard was persistent.

'Sure, when I've applied rule number two, but not today. I'm to bring the sled back to the pitchblende site.'

'Can I come with you when you do come back?'

'That's possible.'

'Promise?'

'No. I just said it was possible, Bonnard, and that's what I mean.'

'I'm never going to learn anything on this trip if I don't get out and do *some* field work, away from screens and . . .'

'If we brought you back to the ship with a part or parts missing, left in the maw of a fringe or a flier, your mother would give up the deep six. So be quiet.' Varian used a sharper tone than she normally employed with Bonnard but his insistence, his air that he had only to wheedle enough and his wish would be granted, annoyed her. She was sympathetic to his irritation with constant restrictions. To the ship-born, planets gave illusions of safety because ship-learned dangers were insulated from one by an atmosphere miles deep, whereas in space only thin metal shells prevented disaster and any broaching of that shell was lethal. No shell, no danger in simplistic terms.

'Would you run through that tape, Bonnard, and see if we have good takes on the fringies,' she asked him after a long pause, mutinous on his part, firm on hers. 'There's something I want to check out with Trizein when we get back to camp. Fardles, but I wish we had access to the EV's data banks.'

After another long pause during which she heard the slight whir of rapidly spun tapes, Bonnard spoke. 'You know, those fliers remind me of something I've seen before. I can almost see the printed label on the tape sleeve . . .'

'What about this tape?'

'Oh, clear pictures, Varian.'

'They've reminded me of something, too, Bonnard, but I can't drag it out of storage either.'

'My mother always says that if you're worrying over something, go to sleep thinking about it and you'll remember in the morning,' said Terilla.

'Good idea, Terilla. I'll do so and so can you, Bonnard. Meanwhile, we're over new territory again. Man the telltale.'

They got some good tags on a stumpy-legged ruminant, spotted but couldn't tag more small mammals like Dandy, and surprised several flocks of scavengers at their work. They returned to the mining site just as the 'gloom thickened', as

Terilla put it. Kai was waiting wih Dimenon and Margit with the equipment which the sled must transport.

'It's a very rich find, Varian,' said Dimenon. He looked very tired and immensely satisfied. He started to add more but stopped, turning to Kai.

'And the next valley over shows another saddle deposit as large and as rich,' said Kai, a grin creasing his sweat and dirt smeared face.

'And probably the next one beyond that,' said Margit, sighing wearily. 'Only that can wait until tomorrow.'

'EV should have given us at least one remote scanner, Kai,' said Dimenon, as he helped load the instruments. This sounded to Varian like the continuation of an argument.

'I requisitioned one, standard. Supply said they'd no more in stock. If you'll remember, we passed quite a few promising systems in the last standard year.'

'When I think of the slogging we'd be saved . . .'

'I dunno,' said Margit, interrupting Dimenon. She placed a coil of wire on the sled deck. 'We do so raking much by remote. I know I've done something today.' She groaned. 'I feel it in every bone and in muscles I didn't know I had. We're soft. No wonder the heavy-worlders sneer at us.'

'Them!' A world of scorn was expressed in Dimenon's single word.

Kai and Varian exchanged quick glances.

'I know they were bloody hungover or something earlier on, but I was glad enough of Paskutti's muscle this afternoon,' Margit went on, pulling herself into the sled and settling down beside Terilla. 'Get in, Di, I'm dying for a wash, and I bloody hope that Portegin's de-odourizer has fixed the water stink. Hydro-telluride does not enhance the body beautiful. So how did you pass the day, scamp?' she asked Terilla.

While the three young people kept a conversation going, Varian wondered, as she set the sled on its baseward course, just what happened to occasion Dimenon's captious attitude. Perhaps it was no more than irritation with the heavy-worlder's behaviour in the morning, and reaction to the excitement of such a rich find. She must ask Kai later. She

94

didn't want her team coming into contention with his, and she would be the first to admit the heavy-worlders had been less than efficient. Or was Dimenon still irked over last night's alcohol rationing?

There were dangers inherent in mixing planet- and ship-bred groups and EV kept it down to a minimum whenever possible. The Iretan expedition had needed the brawn of the heavy-worlders and Varian and Kai would simply have to work out the problems.

Varian was a bit depressed. A computer could give you a probability index on any situation. This mission had had a good one. But a computer couldn't adjust its input with such unexpected details as a stink and constant gloom or drizzle affecting tempers or a cosmic storm cutting off communications with the mother ship: it certainly hadn't printed out the fact that a planet listed as unexplored was now giving immutable evidence of previous survey, not to mention anomalies like . . . But if, Varian thought, there had been the survey, maybe such things as pentadactyl development and aquatic collapsing parallelograms were entirely possible! Yet which was indigenous? Both couldn't be!

Fliers having to find grass so far from their natural habitat? Varian's spirits lifted again with excitement. And if the golden fliers, who were pentadactyl, were *not* indigenous, then the herbivores and predators they'd so far encountered were not indigenous either! Not anomalies: conundrums. And how? By whom? The Others? No, not the ubiquitous Others. They destroyed all life, if there were any substance to the rumour that such sentient beings existed.

The Theks might know about the previous survey . . . if Kai could generate them into a serious attempt at recall. By Matter! She'd sit through an interchange herself to find out! Wait till she told Kai that!

CHAPTER SIX

Kai had as much to reflect upon as Varian as he sledded back to the encampment. For one thing, he was minus some irreplaceable equipment which Paskutti and Tardma had dropped down a crevice. EV had allowed him only the minimum of seismic spares and the last group he'd expect to be careless with equipment were the heavy-worlders. They moved so deliberately they avoided most accidents. He couldn't restrict the heavy-worlders from drinking the distillation but he'd have to ask Lunzie to dilute any given them from now on. He couldn't afford more losses.

An expeditionary force was permitted so many credits in loss of equipment due to unforeseeable accidents but above that figure, the leaders found their personal accounts docked. The loss of the equipment was bothering Kai more than any possible credit subtraction: it was a loss caused by sheer negligence. That irritated him. And his irritation annoyed him more because this should have been a day of personal and team satisfaction: he had achieved what he had been sent to do. Ruthlessly now he suppressed negative feelings.

Beside him Gaber was chattering away in the best spirits the cartographer had exhibited since landing. Berru and Triv were discussing the next day's work in terms of which of the coloured lakes would be the richest in ore-minerals. Triv was wishing for just one remote sensor, with a decent infra-red eye to pierce the everlasting clouds. A week's filming in a polar orbit and the job would be done.

'We do have the probe's tapes,' Berru said.

'That only sounded land mass and ocean depth. No definition, no infra-red to penetrate that eternal cloud cover.'

'I asked for a proper pre-landing remote sensing,' Gaber said, the note of petulance back in his voice.

'So did I,' said Kai, 'and was told there wasn't a suitable satellite in stores. We have to do it the hard way, in person.'

'That would seem to be the criterion for this expedition,' said Gaber, giving Kai a sly glance. 'Everything's done the hard way.'

'You've gone soft, Gaber, that's all,' said Triv. 'Not enough time in the grav gym on shipboard. I enjoy the challenge, frankly. I've gone flabby. This trip's good for all of us. We're spoiled with a punch-a-button-dial-a-comfort system. We need to get back to nature, test our sinews, circulate our blood and . . .'

'Breath deeply of stinking air?' asked Gaber when Triv, carried away by his own eloquence, briefly faltered.

'What, Gaber? Lost your nose filters again?'

Gaber was easy to tease and Triv continued in a bantering way until Kai turned the sled through the gap in the hills to their encampment. Kai had affected not to acknowledge Gaber's glance although, tied in with Gaber's notion of planting, 'doing everything the hard way' could well be a prelude to the abandonment that was euphemistically termed 'planting'. It could account for quite a number of deletions in Kai's original requisition list. Remote sensors were expensive equipment to leave behind with a planted colony. But, if the colony were supposed to be self-sufficient, surely some mining equipment would have been included so that they could refine needed metals for buildings and for replacement of worn-out parts, like sled members. There would have been . . . 'Do it the hard way' rang ominously in Kai's mind. He'd better have a long chat with Varian as soon as he could.

However, *if* this expedition were genuine – the urgent need for the transuranics was a chronic condition in the FPS – then someone, if not their own ARTC-10 EV, would strip the message from the beamer satellite, and take the appropriate action of returning to Ireta to extract the all-important ores and minerals and, incidentially, rescue them. The positive thought encouraged Kai, and he employed the rest of the trip by formulating messages; first to the Thek and then for the long distance capsule. No, he'd only the one capsule. Two large deposits did not really constitute dispatching it. So, first he would frame a message for his next contact with the Thek about the old cores, and the uranium deposits. He would hold the ldc until he could justify its trip. He'd no genuine cause for alarm, apart from a vague suspicion of an ageing cartographer.

To his surprise, the heavy-worlders who had left the site considerably before him to return by lift-belt, had not arrived at the compound. The other sleds had all returned safely. The youngsters were cosseting Dandy while Lunzie watched. She used her over-seeing as an excuse not to answer the importunities of Portegin and Aulia for more joy juice. He saw neither Varian nor Trizein and had decided she must be in the xeno-chemist's laboratory in the shuttle when the heavy-worlders, in their neat formation, came swooping in from the north. The north? He started towards the veil lock to ask Paskutti about such a detour when Varian hailed him from the shuttle. She sounded excited so he hurried over, leaving Paskutti till another time.

'Kai, Trizein thinks he knows why the fliers must need the grasses,' she said when he got near enough. 'The stuff is full of carotene . . . Vitamin A. They must need it for eyesight and pigmentation.'

'Odd that they'd have to go such a distance for a basic requirement.'

'But it substantiates my hunch that the pentadactyls are *not* indigenous to this world.'

Kai was lifting his foot through the iris and stopped, grabbing at the sides to balance himself.

'Not indigenous? What in the name of raking . . . what do you mean? They have to be indigenous. They're here.'

'They didn't originate here,' and Varian gestured him to come into the shuttle. 'Further, those parallelograms I saw today aren't even vaguely arthropods, which would fit in with the vertebrates we've discovered like the herbivores, predators and even the fliers.'

'You're not making any sense.'

'I am. This planet isn't. You don't find animals forced to go hundreds of kilometres from their proper environment to acquire a dietary necessity. What is essential to them is generally supplied right where they live!'

'Now, wait a minute, Varian. Think. If your pentadactyls are not indigenous, they were brought here. Who, why would anyone, want to relocate animals as large as that predator or your Mabel?'

She regarded him steadily, as if she expected him to know the answer to his question.

'You should know. They've already tipped us off. The Theks, slow-top,' she said with some asperity when he remained silent. 'The inscrutable Theks. They've been here before. They left those seismic devices.'

'That makes no sense, Varian.'

'It makes a lot of sense.'

'What reason could the Theks possibly have for such an action?'

'They've probably forgotten,' Varian said, grinning mischievously. 'Along with the fact that they'd surveyed this planet before.'

They had reached Trizein's lab and he was contemplating the enlarged image of some fibres.

'Of course, we'd need to have one of those avians of yours, Varian, to discover if it requires carotene,' Trizein was saying as if he didn't realize that Varian had left the lab.

'We've Mabel,' said Varian, 'and little Dandy.'

'You've animals in this compound?' Trizein blinked with astonishment.

'I told you we had, Trizein. The slides you analyzed yesterday and the day before . . .'

'Ah, yes, I remember now,' but it was obvious to his listeners that he didn't remember any such thing.

'Mabel and Dandy aren't fliers,' Kai said. 'They're completely different species.'

'Indeed they are, but they are also pentadactyl. So is the fang-face and *he* needed the grasses.'

'Mabel and Dandy are herbivorous,' said Kai, 'and the predator and the fliers aren't.'

Varian considered that qualification. 'Yes, but generally

speaking, carnivores absorb sufficient Vitamin C from the animals they eat who do get it regularly in their diet.' She shook her head over the quandary. 'Then fang-face wouldn't need to go to the valley. He'd get enough from chewing Mabel's flank. I don't make any sense out of it – yet. Besides, the fliers may have another reason for gathering grass, as Terilla pointed out today.'

'You've lost me,' said Kai, and then directed Varian's attention to Trizein who had gone back to his microscope viewer and was oblivious to their presence again.

'You'll understand when you see the tapes we got today of those fliers, Kai. C'mon, unless you've got something else to do?'

'Frame messages to the Theks but let me see what you taped first.'

'By the way, Kai,' said Varian following him out of the lab, 'we didn't encounter any life-forms in the vicinity of the pitchblende saddle that would cause a secondary camp there any trouble. If the camp's set up properly, and preferably on a prominence and the force-screen posted deep, your team should be safe enough.'

'That's good news. Not that I think you'd've scared anyone off with tales of herds of fang-faces.'

'Fang-faces, for the record, are solitary hunters.'

They had reached the pilot cabin and Varian inserted the tape for playback, explaining her conclusions and her desire to investigate the golden furred fliers' colony more closely at the earliest opportunity.

'How closely, Varian?' asked Kai. 'They're not small and, as I remember, those wings are strong and could be dangerous. I'd hate to get attacked by that beak.'

'So would I. So I'm not going to be. I'll go slowly, Kai, but if they're as intelligent as the evidence suggests, I may even be able to approach them on a personal basis.' When Kai began to protest, she held up her hand. 'The fliers are not stupid like Mabel, or scared like Dandy, or dangerous like fang-face. But I cannot give up the opportunity to investigate an aerial species that acts in such an organized manner.'

'Fair enough, but do nothing on your own, co-leader. I want heavy-worlders with you at all times.'

'You're a friend! Did they improve with the day?'

'I've never seen them so clumsy: slow, yes, but never plain raking grease-fingered. Paskutti and Tardma dropped one of the seismimics down a crevice. I don't have so many that I can spare one,' said Kai, 'not if I'm to complete my survey.' He shook his head again over the loss. I'm not blaming you, or them; but it is a nuisance. And what are we going to do about that fruit distillation? I don't understand why it should have affected them so adversely when we weaker types had no trouble?'

'It might not have been the drink.'

'What do you mean?'

Varian shrugged. 'Just a notion. Nothing specific.'

'Then let us find a specific, and have Lunzie run a few tests. It might be a mutational allergy. Say, did you send the heavy-worlders on any errands today? In the north?'

'North? No. They were at your disposal today. Now, about the pitchblende site? You'll be working from there again tomorrow? Okay, then I'll send a team in for a ground check. There seem to be only smaller animals not, as I've told the youngsters, that size is any indication of potential danger. What other area do you want us to check out xenobiologically as a possible secondary base?'

Kai tapped out of the computer the print of Gaber's chart, updated now with the pitchblende site and the old cores.

'The shield edge is only two hundred kilometres from here in the north-west so we won't need a secondary camp there yet. But Portegin and Aulia want to examine these lakes and go further into this flatland area. Berru and Triv are scheduled to go due west where there appears to be a wide continental basin. Might have petroleum pools: not as rich an energy source, naturally, but crude oil has uses. We might be able to refine enough to use as an auxiliary fuel for the . . .'

'Kai, did anyone use the big sled for any length of time this morning?'

'Just to reach the site. Then it was turned over to you. Why?'

'Because its elapsed flight time is longer than it should have been. Damned thing's due now for a power change.'

'So?'

'I dunno. Just that I don't usually make errors in my figures.'

'We've enough worries, Varian, without imagining more.'

Varian grimaced. 'Like no contact with EV. Your teams'll be expecting some acknowledgement . . .'

'We've got some leeway, and I'll use every day of it.'

'Yes, we do have stall time, don't we. By the way, those youngsters were very useful to me. I think I'll opt them again when I don't need to land,' she hastily added as she saw the objections forming in Kai's startled face. 'You might even consider,' and she grinned slyly, 'taking Bonnard with you on a coring expedition.'

'Now just a minute, Varian . . .'

'They do say that over-exposure cures a lot of fancies.'

'True. How about helping me with that message to the Theks?'

'Sorry, Kai, I've got to release Mabel, check with Lunzie and get a wash before eating.' Varian quickly opened the iris. 'But I'd be happy to look over what you plan to say.'

He made as if to throw something at her but she scampered away, laughing.

An hour later, he was certain that Varian at her worst could have constructed a better message to the Theks. It covered the main points, and requested the return information required.

He beamed the message, confirming a contact hour two days' later. It didn't give Theks much time to meditate their answers but he had specified only yes, no or deferred answers.

The next day went as scheduled, the heavy-worlders restored to operating efficiency. Tardma and Tanegli did a ground survey of the densely vegetated area where small life forms had been telltagged by Varian and the youngsters. The creatures had maintained their anonymity but skeletal remains not yet disintegrated by insect and carrion eater indicated that while carnivorous, the creatures were probably nocturnal hunters and not large enough to constitute a real danger. Further, they were unlikely to be caught so far from their own territory as the secondary camp. Kai spent the afternoon with Dimenon and Margit choosing a site. It was decided that Portegin and Aulia could also use the camp for their westerly investigations.

Lunzie told Kai and Varian confidentially that the heavy-worlders ought to have had a higher tolerance for the fruit drink than the light grav or ship-bred. She couldn't understand their reactions. However, she did not recommend rationing or watering the potion. She could bring the heavy-worlders in for a routine physical, which, she allowed, was a good idea for every member of the expedition, to check on any allergenic tendencies or subtle infections acquired since planetfall.

That evening Lunzie supplied enough of the fruit drink to make the evening extremely convivial. The heavy-worlders drank no more than anyone else, laughed infrequently as was their habit and retired when everyone else did. The following day there was no impairment of their efficiency which increased the mystery of their behaviour that first evening.

The contact hour with the Theks was duly kept by Kai. Varian arrived half-way through the ponderous and slowly delivered reply.

'No' was the answer to his questions about messages being stripped from the satellite and contact with the EV. He received the expectable deferred answer concerning any knowledge of previous survey and the discovery of the old cores. Excellent was their response to news of the pitchblende deposit, with 'continue' added. To his comment that he had heard from the Ryxi he got an acknowledgement. The Theks were reputedly tolerant of all species in a benevolent, impartial way but Kai was left with the feeling that the Theks couldn't care less if the Ryxi maintained contact.

He was of two minds about their deferred answer on a previous survey. On one hand, he'd half-hoped they could find a previous reference, though how they could, out of contact with their own kind and EV's data banks, he didn't know. On the other hand, he would have been obscurely relieved if they had proved their fallability. Yet, if this case did shatter their reputation, something stable and secure would be lost forever to him.

'So they don't know,' said Varian, blatantly pleased.

'Not actively at any rate,' he replied, quite willing to take the Thek part to offset his mental disloyalty. 'Of course, there are only several million planets in the universe on which life of some sort has evolved . . .'.

'So we're constantly informed but our sphere of interest is currently limited to this one stinking ball of earth. By the way, in order to set you up a secondary camp, we're going to have to formulate a few plans,' said Varian. 'According to the old core pattern, the shield runs about two thousand kilometres in a long point to the south-east. That makes commuting back here unfeasible. I want to take Tanegli, Paskutti, Tardma and Lunzie and check out that area.' She unrolled area charts, some of the topographical features already marked out in Gaber's neat draftsmanship. Over these were wash colours, the key at the side. 'I've keyed it here to territorialities of the beasts we've tagged. I think the guide is adequate but there is so much animal life in this area,' and she indicated the plateau and rain forest just beyond the dead parameters of the camp, 'that I've only bothered with the big and dangerous ones. Here's a spot frame of each type we've observed enough to identify as herbivorous, carnivorous or omnivorous. As you can see, we've a way to go before we've done even the most superficial cataloguing.' She tapped vast areas of the outlined land mass which were pristine. 'Here there be dragons!' she added in a fruity voice.

'Dragons?'

'Well, that's what the antique cartographer would say when they didn't know a binary bit about the indigenous life.'

'Any more news on which species is which here?' asked Kai.

She shook her head, handing him several copies of the maps. 'That's not as urgent as your geological work, and you needed some sort of a guide.'

'This map is terrific, Varian. I thought you'd been out with your teams ...'

'No, I sent them to get me this information, and fill in some of the nearby gaps in our survey. Terilla and I collaborated on the composite.'

'Terilla did these with you?' Impressed, Kai was poring over the charts.

'Yes, indeed. I know the youngsters were sort of dumped on us at the last moment but I wish someone had thought to give us their records. Terilla's been a real find and she could have been apprenticed right off to Gaber and kept him from falling so far behind. He even approves of her work.' Varian grinned saucily at Kai. 'You'll be relieved to hear that Bonnard's interest has been transferred.'

'To Dandy? Or Mabel? In neither case am I flattered.'

'Mabel's long gone. No, Bonnard is aiming to get on my expedition to the golden fliers.'

'At least he picks something demonstrably intelligent.'

'I never said he didn't have good taste.'

'Varian!'

'When's the contact with the Ryxi?'

'This afernoon at 15.30 hours. If they remember.'

'We do have problems with memory this trip, don't we? The Ryxi remembering to speak to us, the Theks remembering to think and EV remembering to get in touch with us. Well, back to my hot drawing board ...' She started out of the pilot cabin. 'Oh, hello, Gaber ...'

'Varian, did you take all my chart copies?'

'Except the one Terilla was working on. Why?'

'I didn't know. I just didn't know and I was ...'

'I did tell you, Gaber, but I guess you were so deep in the tape, you didn't hear me. Sorry about that. I've given Kai copies, and I'm on my way back to your lair with these right now.'

'Oh, very well then. And, if I didn't hear you, I am sorry.'

To Kai, Gaber did not sound the least bit sorry. Kai went back to studying the patterns of animal. The biggest herbivores, like Mabel and three other large types, could be found all through the rain forests, with their probable passages through the mountain ranges neatly designated by tiny drawings of the beasts. The predators, like fang-face, hunted singly: only one pair had been discovered and they had been involved in a ferocious battle, which had deteriorated, in Paskutti's words, into a mating. The scope of the charts was hampered by the large uncharted areas, over which a transparency had been laid, indicating the general topographical features as seen by the initial cursory probe.

They had been concentrating on the relatively cooler portion of the shield mass, since the polar region was much hotter than the equatorial due to the hotter thermal core of the planet. They would soon have to penetrate those steaming jungles, a task Kai did not relish. The proliferation and diversity of life forms would be incredible in such warmth, Varian had warned him during their shipboard briefing sessions. The lush tropical jungles nourished life, provided quantities of food, as well as immense competition for any and all edible substances. In cooler climates, though Ireta could not boast a very temperate zone, there tended to be fewer species since the food supply was limited by the more severe conditions of life.

With understandable satisfaction, Kai took his own maps and marked in the two pitchblende finds, and those of the day before when Portegin and Aulia had sited two large copper deposits, and Berru and Triv had marked three mountains of iron ores. Whoever had been here before had denuded the shield areas but plate action in the ensuing milleniums had made the unstable areas doubly rich. This was actually Kai's first search expedition: his other assignments had been remedial – finding veins which had faulted out, or flooding controls and deep sea manganese dredging: all valuable experience and designed to aid him in a full scale planetary survey like this one.

He was so deep in his thoughts that the warning of his chrono jerked him to attention and bewilderment as to why he had had the alarm set.

The Ryxi contact! Belatedly he realized that he should

have prepared a message for them. It was easier to read a written message fast than gabble spontaneously at the speed required for the Ryxi. He jotted down some notes as the communication unit warmed to its task. Diplomatically he phrased Varian's comments about the golden fliers.

Vrl came on as scheduled, asking for confirmation of contact with EV. Kai replied in the negative but Vrl did not seem too concerned. He said that they had sent their full report by long distance capsule to their home world. He intimated that he didn't care how long it took to arrive, he and his group were well and pleasantly established. Kai had half a mind not to say anything about the golden fliers if Vrl didn't ask. But the avian did. Kai told him the little Varian and he had observed. Luckily he had the tape on for Vrl's excited reply erupted in Kai's ears at an articulate speed. Kai got the impression that he was a lying discontent, envious of the Ryxi and making the whole species up. Vrl signed off before Kai could vindicate himself or arrange another contact time.

He was staring, bemused and somewhat aggravated by Vrl's over-reaction when he heard the sound of a cleared throat. Gaber was standing in the iris lock.

'I'm sorry to intrude, Kai, but we are missing one of the area maps. Do you have two copies of one there?'

Kai fingered the tough but thin sheets. They did stick together occasionally when the copying solution dried. 'No, I've only the one set.'

'Well, then a set is missing,' said Gaber in his customary aggrieved tone and left.

Kai could see him shaking his head as he made for the shuttle's lock. Kai set the communicator for a slow replay of the interchange with Vrl, vowing that Varian ought to do an intensive study of those fliers as soon as possible.

CHAPTER SEVEN

In the next seven days, the expedition was too busy setting up the secondary camps to indulge in any activity not strictly necessary to these primary aims. Varian found time to return to the fish rock and bring several small dessicated specimens of the fringes for Trizein to study. The man buried himself in his laboratory until Lunzie found him asleep at his work desk. She forced him to take a break, eat and sleep. He did so unwillingly and when he woke, he stumbled about the compound with unseeing eyes, though he did stop once to stare at Dandy with a puzzled expression.

The little creature was quite tame and permitted out of its run when Bonnard and Cleiti were on hand. Varian had decided not to release it as, orphaned, it had no natural protector. Kai had to accede to her arguments since it was obvious the little beast would never reach a great size and was therefore no strain on the expedition's time or resources. Dandy was, by nature, timid and content to follow the youngsters about, its large liquid eyes wistful or startled by turns. Kai would privately have preferred more of an extrovert personality in a tamed beast but Dandy posed no problem of aggressive behaviour. Kai still thought it a very nondescript affair.

The golden fliers were continually seen in the skies, almost as if, Varian said one evening, they were as interested in the new occupants of their skies as the expedition was in them. She had been gleefully enchanted by Vrl's reaction to their existence for, as the slow playback confirmed, the Ryxi had spluttered out a repudiation of Varian's report, indicating that an intelligent avian species was unlikely to occur again on any planet, under any conditions: the Ryxi were unique and would remain so and any attempt to supplant their preeminent position in the Federation would be met by severe measures. Vrl suggested that this was a hoax which the

108

bipeds had better forget, retract and abandon or he would recommend that all contact between Ryxi and Human be forthwith severed.

Once Terilla's animal maps were circulated, Tanegli and Gaber vyed with each other for her time and skill to the point where Varian and Kai had to intervene. Unconcerned by such competition for her assistance, Terilla made it quite plain that she much preferred plants to charts or animals. Chuckling, Varian showed Kai the map the girl had inscribed for Tanegli indicating the position of flora, grass and shrub on the plains and swamp areas. A work schedule was evolved in which Terilla spent three afternoons with each man while her morning hours were hers. With increased work loads, Kai assigned tasks to Bonnard and Cleiti as he would any other member of the expedition. Tanegli usually opted for Bonnard and Cleiti when Terilla was not available for his botanical excursions. Sometimes Bonnard acted as recorder for Bakkun when administration duties prevented Kai from field-work beside the heavy-world geologist.

Lunzie annexed Cleiti on those days to help her test Ireta's soil and vegetation for any unusual medicinal properties.

Two secondary camps were sited and occupied but it was obvious that a third camp to the far east would have to be established to continue exploration of the easterly land mass. Kai projected that over half their expeditionary time would be spent in the eastern hemisphere. He hoped that the fifteen degree axial tilt would mean some cooler weather in the polar regions when the teams had to move to complete the survey in the western hemisphere.

On neither of his next two contacts with the Theks did they have any good news for him of the deferred query or of the EV. Kai's leeway on the matter of response from EV was fast running out. He was prepared and had Varian's support when Dimenon forced an admission of a contact lapse. Kai cited the cosmic storm in such an off-handed manner that Dimenon never thought to ask if the ores report was the only message uncollected.

'How long a grace period we have now, I wouldn't estimate,' Kai told Varian afterwards.

'Keep 'em so busy counting their paydirt bonuses that they'll forget to ask.'

'This is a raking rich planet, Varian.'

'So? It's up to EV to stay in touch with us, if they want the energy materials we've found. They know where we are.' Varian held Kai's gaze and she jerked up one eyebrow. 'You aren't considering Gaber's ludicrous notion, are you?'

'It does occur to me now and then,' Kai said, rubbing the side of his nose, feeling silly but actually relieved to hear Varian air the matter.

'Hmmm, yes. It occurs to me now and then, too. Have the Ryxi reported in again?'

'No.' Kai grinned at her. 'Did you expect them to?'

'No.' She laughed. 'They are so . . . pompously paranoiac. As if another intelligent avian could possibly threaten them. I mean, the giffs,' which was the nickname she'd given the golden fliers, '*are* intelligent but so far from the Ryxi position that it's asinine for them to take umbrage.' Varian sighed. 'I'd love to evaluate their intelligence.'

'Why don't you?'

'With your lot agitating for that eastern camp?'

'What about next rest day? Make a small start. Go observe them, relax for the day.'

'Could I?' Varian brightened at the prospect. 'Could I take the big sled, sleep out in it? We've got their flight habits well documented now, we've caught the fishing act often enough to establish that drill, but I don't know much about their personal life, their matutinal habits. And there's only the one place for those grasses they eat. They do use swamp grass for net-weaving but I don't know exactly how they accomplish the feat.' She gave him a sideways frown. 'You need a break as much as I do. Let's both go, next rest day. Paskutti and Lunzie can sub for us.'

'What if we arrive on the giff rest day?' asked Kai with a very bland expression.

'There's always that possibility, isn't there?' she replied, not taking his lure.

Kai was astonished at how eagerly he looked forward to the break in routine. That showed how right Varian had been in suggesting it. Lunzie approved wholeheartedly, telling Kai she'd been about to recommend a day off for them both. She wasn't too sure that observing the giffs at close range constituted a proper holiday but the physician was equally keen to know more about the giffs.

'What is there about winged creatures that fascinates us all?' Lunzie asked as they sat about after the evening meal over beakers of distilled fruit juice.

'Their independence?' asked Kai.

' "If we had been meant to fly, we'd've been given wings," ' quipped Varian in a thin nasal voice, then continued in a normal tone, 'I suspect it is the freedom, or perhaps the view, the perspective, the feeling of infinite space about you. You ship-bred types can't appreciate open spaces the way the planet-bred can, but I do need vistas on which to feast my eyes, and soul.'

'Confinement, voluntary or involuntary, can have adverse effects on temperament and psychology, resulting in serious maladjustments,' Lunzie said. 'One reason why we include the youngsters on planetfall assignments as often as possible.'

Kai remained silent, acutely conscious of his own sometimes pressing agoraphobia.

'We have surrogate wings,' Lunzie continued, 'in the agency of sleds and lift-belts . . .'

'Which do not quite produce the same freedoms,' said Kai slowly, wondering what it would feel like to be independent of all artificial aids: to dip, dive, soar and glide without the unconscious restrictive considerations of fuel, stress, metal fatigue.

'Why, Kai,' said Varian, regarding him with delighted astonishment, 'you're the last one I'd expect to understand.'

'Perhaps,' he said with a wry smile, 'you planet-bred types underestimate the ship-bred.'

Dimenon, who'd been in an uproariously good mood that

111

evening, since he and Margit had flown in to report finding not only a stream running with gold nuggets but the parent lode, had brought out his handpiano. He began to render a boisterous ballad with interminable verses and a silly syllabic chorus with such an infectious tune that everyone joined in. To Kai's surprise, so did the heavy-worlders, thumping the plasfloor with their heavy boots and clapping with unusual enthusiasm.

Margit wanted to dance and dragged Kai onto the floor, yelling at Dimenon to leave off the endless verses and play some decent music. Kai was never certain when the heavy-worlders disappeared but the convivial gathering lasted well past the rise of the third moon.

He awoke suddenly the next morning, with an urgency that suggested danger. When he scrambled out of the sleeping sack to the window of his dome, the scene was quiet. Dandy was sprawled asleep in his pen. There was no movement. The day had started, the brighter patch of cloud which was the sun was well above the soft slope of the eastern hills. Whatever had alarmed his subconscious was not apparent.

He was roused and so keyed up by the abrupt triggering that he decided to remain up. He dragged on a clean ship suit, inserted a fresh lining in his boots and fastened them. He had a small larder in his dome and broke open a wake-up beaker, reminding himself to check with Lunzie today on the state of the stores. He could not shake his sensation that something was amiss so he did a tour of the encampment.

There wasn't a smell of smoke in the main dome. Gaber was fast asleep in his, the windows were opaqued in the other sleeping quarters so he did not intrude. Remembering Trizein's tendency to work through a night, he made his way quickly to the shuttle craft, waving open the iris lock. The conditioned air inside gave him pause. Suddenly he realized that he hadn't put his nose filters in: and he hadn't *smelled* Ireta!

'Muhlah! I'm getting used to it.' His soft exclamation echoed in the bare main cabin of the shuttle. Kai walked quietly back to Trizein's lab, opened the iris and peered in.

Some experiments were in progress, judging by the activity of dials and gauges in the built-in equipment but Trizein's form on the ledge-bed was motionless.

As Kai turned from the lab, he noticed that the supply hold iris was open. He must caution Trizein about that. Lunzie kept her decanted fruit brew in there. Kai had noticed conspicuous consumption the night before and his aggressiveness when Margit suggested he'd had enough. Kai didn't quite put it past the man to appropriate a flask for evening use in the secondary camp. Not a habit he'd approve or condone in any of his team members.

Although his inspection satisfied him that nothing was demonstrably wrong, his uneasiness remained until, after returning to his dome, he became immersed in the restricted file in the ship's data bank. By the time the rest of the expedition was stirring, he had rid himself of the backlog of detail. The inadvertently early rising had been rewarding.

Dimenon, looking untouched by the previous evening's carousal, arrived in the main dome with Margit, both suited up and ready to return to their base. They ate quickly, wanting to make an early start back, but as they were leaving, Dimenon asked Kai when he expected to contact the Theks again. He did not seem disturbed when Kai gave a time three days later.

'Well, let us know how EV appreciates our labours on this stinking planet. Although—' Dimenon frowned and felt his nostrils, 'Rake it! I forgot to put 'em in again!'

'Smell anything?' asked Kai, amused.

Dimenon's eyes began to widen and his mouth dropped in exaggerated reaction.

'I've got used to the stench!' He roared the statement, full of aggrieved incredulity. 'Kai, please, when you've got through to EV, have them pick us up before schedule? Please, I've got used to the stench of hydro-telluride.' He clutched at his throat now, contorting his face as though in terminal agony, 'I can't stand it. I can't stand it.'

Lunzie, who was literal minded, came rushing up, frowning with anxiety while Kai tried to gesture reassurance. Others were grinning at Dimenon's histrionics but the heavy-worlders, after uninterested glances at the geologist, turned back to their own quiet-toned discussions. Lunzie still hadn't realized that Dimenon was acting. He grabbed at her shoulders now.

'Tell me, Lunzie, tell me I'm not a goner. My sense of smell'll come back, won't it. Once I'm in decent air? Oh, don't tell me I'll never be able to smell nothing in the air again . . .'

'If the acclimitization should be permanent, you could always get an Iretan air-conditioning for your shipboard quarters,' Lunzie replied, apparently in earnest.

Dimenon looked horrified and, for a moment, didn't catch the brand of the physician's humour.

'C'mon, partner, you've been bested,' said Margit, taking him by the arm. 'Better to smell the sweet air of another find . . .'

'*Could* you get so used to Iretan stink you'd never smell normal again?' Bonnard asked Lunzie, a little worried as he watched the two geologists leave.

'No,' said Lunzie with a dry chuckle. 'The smell is powerful but I doubt there's any permanent desensitization. The temporary effect *is* somewhat of a blessing. Do you have it?'

Bonnard nodded uncertainly. 'But I didn't know I couldn't smell it anymore until Dimenon mentioned it.' This worried him.

'Since you are now used to the overbearing smell, see if you can now distinguish other, previously unsensed odours, while you're out and about today.'

'Worse ones?' Bonnard regarded Lunzie, appalled.

'I can smell a difference in the blossoms I've been cataloguing,' said Terilla. 'And some of the leaves have an odour if you crush 'em. Not too bad a smell, really,' she added helpfully.

That morning Kai checked with Lunzie about stores. She was not the sort of person to give spot replies and together they went to the store hold.

'I'm not missing any of the fruit distillation, if that's what

114

you're worried about, Kai,' she said in her direct fashion. 'We've not made too many inroads in the subsistence supplies, either. I've been gradually phasing them out entirely, in favour of local protein.'

'You have?' Kai was surprised.

'You hadn't noticed?' There was a slight emphasis on the pronoun. Lunzie smiled briefly with pleasure at the success of her programme. 'We are losing hard goods, though, at a rate which worries me.'

'Hard goods?'

'Knives, film and sheet extruders, spare charges for life-belts . . .'

'What did the secondary camps take?'

'Not enough to account for some of these items. Unless, of course, they haven't reported the losses and have merely helped themselves when I was busy elsewhere.' That solution sounded plausible. 'If I may, I'll appoint Cleiti as requisitions officer and have her on hand when anyone needs to visit the supply hold. We can keep a check that way without giving offence . . .'

'Or warning,' thought Kai, and then decided that his imagination was working overtime. He did need that day's respite.

Varian returned to the camp from one of her search and identity sweeps early in the afternoon before rest day. She cornered Kai in his dome, scornfully clacking the tape holders that were stacked in front of him, tugging at the seismic print-out on the volcanic action in the north-west which he had been studying. Pressures were mounting on a long trans-form fault and he was hoping they'd have enough warning to be able to observe the earthquake when the phenomenon occurred.

'Leave that, Kai. You can zip through report work a lot faster with a fresh mind.'

'It's early yet . . .'

'Raking right it is. I got back special so I could pry you out of here before the teams come in and dump such glowing reports on you that you feel obliged to listen.' She went back to the iris lock. 'Cleiti! Did you organize those supplies for us? And where's Bonnard?' The reply was inaudible to Kai but satisfactory to Varian who nodded. 'If he's sure he's got what he needs, tell him to pack it into the sled beside my things. Kai, where's your pack? Ha! Thought so. Okay, what do you need?'

Varian moved purposefully to his storage chest so that Kai pushed back his stool and waved her away. She stood, grinning but adamant, while he packed what he needed into his sleep sack, and gathered up his safety gear. With a courteous sweep of his hand, he indicated he was ready.

'I knew I'd have to haul you out of here.' Varian sounded grimly smug.

'Then what are you dragging your feet for?' asked Kai with a smile and exited before her. As an afterthought, he thumblocked the iris control. He didn't really want anyone to happen across the message tapes with the Theks.

As Varian neatly swung the big sled over the encampment, sparkling with the blue demise of insects, she groaned. 'We should have brought a small unit for tonight. We'll have to sleep in belt screens!'

'Not if we sack out on the sled floor,' said Bonnard, eyeing the space. 'I think there's room enough if we stack our supplies on the front seating and remove the side benches. Shall I activate the telltale?'

'This once, we'll leave it silent,' said Varian. 'There wouldn't be anything untagged this close to camp anyway.'

A companionable silence enveloped the three and lasted the entire trip to the inland sea which they reached just as the last speck of gloom, as Bonnard phrased it, began to fade from the sullen skies. Varian had marked a good landing site, a shallow terrace beyond and below the main congregation of the giffs but with a fine view of the summit where the netted fish were deposited.

The first hour after sunset there was a brief surcease of daytime insect activity before the nocturnal creatures became a menace. During this interim, Varian heated their evening meal on the bare stone terrace. Then, to the amazement of

116

Bonnard and the consternation of Kai, she removed dead branches from the storage section of the sled and lit a small fire.

'Campfire is very comforting even if you ship-bred types think it's atavistic. My father and I used to have one every night on our expeditions.'

'It's very pretty,' said Bonnard in a tentative tone, and looked towards Kai to see his reaction.

Kai smiled and told himself to relax. Fire on shipboard was a hazard: his instant reflex had been to grab something to smother the flames, but as he eyed the small fire, which posed no danger to him, the dancing spikes were pleasantly hypnotic. The small warmth it exuded gave them a circle of light and certainly kept the insects away.

'The oldest belt-screen in the world,' Varian said, poking the fire to fresh vigour with a stick. 'On Protheon, they were particular about their firewoods, choosing those which gave off pleasant aromas. They liked scent with their warmth and light. I wouldn't dare try that on Ireta.'

'Why not?' asked Bonnard, his eyes fixed on a point deep in the flames. 'Terilla said there's some that smell pretty good – by Iretan standards. You know, Varian, I haven't been able to smell anything but Ireta! D'you suppose Lunzie could be wrong and my nose has gone dead?'

Varian and Kai both laughed. 'You'll know soon enough when we get back to the EV,' Varian told him.

'Yeah!' Bonnard's reply lacked any enthusiasm for return.

'You'd be sorry to leave?'

'I sure will, Kai, and it's not because we'll have to leave Dandy. There's so much to do here. I mean, tapes are great, and better than nothing, but this trip I'm learning hundreds of things. Learning's got a point . . .'

'You have to have had the theoretical study before you can attempt the practical,' Varian said but Bonnard waved that consideration aside.

'I've studied basics till data comes out my pores but it isn't the same thing at all as being here and doing it!' Bonnard was emphatically banging his knee. 'Like that fire, and all.

Rakers, on shipboard you see flames and dash for the foamer!'

Varian grinned at Kai and caught his rueful expression.

'Your point's taken, Bonnard,' she said. 'And I think it's safe to say that you'll be in demand for more expeditions once Kai and I have made our report. Bakkun thinks highly of your performance as his recorder.'

'He does?' Bonnard's expression which had soured at the contemplation of return to EV, brightened with such a future. 'You're sure?' His gaze went from Varian to Kai.

'As far as you can be sure of a heavy-worlder.'

'Are there more expeditions planned, Varian?' asked Bonnard urgently.

'More or less,' she replied, catching Kai's gaze. 'I was signed on this tour for three expeditions requiring a xenob over a period of four standard years. You'd be eligible as a junior member in that time. Of course, you might opt for geology rather than xenob.'

'I like animals,' said Bonnard, testing the words in his mouth so as not to give offence to either leader, 'but I do like . . . sort of fancy the more scientific aspects of . . .'

'I'd think you'd be best as an all-round recorder, with as many specialties in that area as possible,' said Varian, helping him.

'You do?'

His reaction made it obvious to Kai and Varian that it was the mechanics of recording that fascinated the boy, rather than any of the individual disciplines. They talked about specialization as the fire burned down, was replenished, and burned down again. By the time Kai suggested they sack out, the two leaders had assured Bonnard that they would give him as much opportunity at tape and recorders as possible to see if this was really where his interests lay.

Safe under the sled's protective screen, they slept deeply and without a bother from the night creatures of Ireta.

Varian was aroused the next morning by something prodding her shoulder. She was still sleepy but again she was prodded, more emphatically this time, and her name was whispered urgently.

'Varian. Varian! Wake up. We got company.'

That forced her to open eyes which she instantly closed, not believing her first sight.

'Varian, you've got to wake up!' Bonnard's whisper was anxious.

'I am. I've seen.'

'What do we do?'

'Have you moved yet?'

'Only to nudge you. Did I hurt?'

'No.' They were both speaking in low tones. 'Can you prod Kai awake?'

'I don't know how he wakes up.'

Bonnard had a point. It wouldn't do to rouse someone who erupted out of the sack like a torpedo. He'd known how to rouse her since he'd often done so when they'd first acquired Dandy.

'Kai's quiet if you do it as gently as you woke me.'

Varian grinned to herself. She wasn't sorry she'd included Bonnard on this trip: last night's discussion had proved how much he'd needed the encouragement as well as the opportunity to talk without reservations imposed on him by the presence of older team members or the two girls. It had been obvious last evening that Kai would have preferred to have made this a duet trip, and a complete break from the exigencies of leadership. Now she'd pried him away from his tape decks, she'd do it again, without a third party.

They had slept head to foot, so while Bonnard prodded Kai's shoulder with his foot, Varian whispered the warning to him.

'Kai, wake slowly, don't move. The observers are observed.'

She had her eyes half-open now, because the giffs were so closely ringed about the sled that, in her first arousal, she had seen a series of bright black eyes on a level with hers.

She almost giggled when a sharp orangey beak point tapped at the plascreen surrounding the sled, tapping gently as if not wishing to startle the sleepers.

'Muhlah!' was Kai's soft curse and there was a ripple of laughter in his tone.

'Is it safe for me to have a look?' asked Bonnard in his hushed whisper.

'Don't know why not. They're looking at us.'

'Can they get in?' was Bonnard's anxious question.

'I doubt it,' said Varian, unperturbed. She wouldn't guarantee that the plascreen could stand a concerted attack of heavier adult beaks but she didn't feel that aggression was the giffs' intent.

'I thought you wanted to see their matutinal habits, Varian,' said Kai, slowly raising his hand from the sleep sack to prop it on his hand. He wasn't looking at her, but beyond her to the golden furred faces peering in.

'That was my intention.'

'As I recall it, I asked you what if it was their rest day?'

Varian couldn't suppress her laughter and Bonnard joined in, never dropping his eyes from the giffs.

'You mean, they're taking the day off to watch us?'

'They're at least starting the day doing it,' said Varian, raising herself slowly out of the sack.

The avians moved restlessly, wings awkwardly held up.

'Hey, they can rotate the wings at the wrist . . .'

'Yes, Bonnard, I'd noticed.' Varian had also seen the flexing of the three digits with the yellowed claws at the tips. The function of thumb and little finger had been incorporated into the wing so Varian couldn't see how they would be able to weave with the three wing digits.

'Hey, they're not all here,' said Bonnard, pointing up in a judiciously controlled gesture.

None of the giffs were perched on top of the plascreen so that the sky was clearly visible. Outlined against the clouds was a formation of giffs going in a south-easterly direction.

'I think we've got the youngsters here,' said Varian.

'The babes at that,' said Kai, pointing to the trail of brownish slime that drippled down the outside skirting of the sled.

Bonnard muffled a chortle. 'So what do we do now? I'm hungry.'

'Then we'll eat,' said Varian and began to pull her legs out of the sack, slowly, to give the giffs no reason for alarm. 'Yes, they're the young ones,' she said as she slowly got to her feet and stared down at the small bodies pressing in about the sled.

Seen in proper perspective, she realized none of these giffs were adult sized. The tip of the longest head crest came only to her waist. She'd estimated that a fully grown giff would be as tall as an average human, with a wing span of at least eight to ten metres.

'What do we do?' asked Bonnard.

'Sit up slowly. I'll bring you breakfast in the sack,' she said, moving carefully to the supplies.

Kai had pulled himself into a sitting position now and gratefully accepted the steaming beaker.

'Breakfast with an audience,' he said, sipping.

'I wish they'd move or talk or something,' said Bonnard, glancing nervously about him as he blew to cool the liquid in his beaker. He almost dropped it when one of the giffs stretched and flapped wings suddenly. 'They're not even trying to get at us.'

'Look but don't touch?' asked Kai. 'Frankly, I'd just as soon they kept to themselves. Those beak points look sharp.' He glanced at Varian who had a small recorder in her hands now, and holding it at waist level was slowly turning a full circle, recording the faces of their audience.

With equal care against sudden movement, she placed the recorder on one shoulder and turning again, stood so still for a long moment at one point that Kai asked what was up.

'I've the recorder directed on the main summit. There's quite a bit of activity here right now. I can't see what it's all about . . . Oh, yes, I do. It's the adults. I'd swear . . . yes . . . they're calling this lot.'

As reluctantly as any curious young creature, the juvenile giffs began to lumber awkwardly away, disappearing so suddenly that Bonnard cried out in alarm.

'They're okay, Bonnard,' said Varian who had a better view. 'We're right on the cliff edge. They've just walked off it and if you'll glance over your shoulder, you'll see them soaring away, perfectly safe.'

'Muhlah!' exclaimed Kai with utter disgust. 'We had 'em close enough and didn't telltag 'em.'

'What? And scare them into bringing momma and dad down on us? We don't really need to telltag giffs anyway, Kai. We know where they live, and how far they range.' She patted the recorder. 'And I've got their faces all on tape.'

'They sure had a good enough look at ours,' said Bonnard. 'I wonder if they'll remember us next time.'

'All furless, crestless faces look the same,' said Varian with a laugh.

She was moving about the sled now without restraint and handed each a bar of subsistence protein. She perched on the pilot chair to munch hers.

When they had finished eating, joking about the manner of their awakening, they made ready to leave the sled. Kai and Bonnard carried the recorders and additional tapes, Varian had her gift of the grasses. Kai also wore a stunner, hoping he wouldn't have to use it. Not, he thought privately, that he'd have much chance the way those giffs could move.

As they emerged, the sun came through the cloud cover, for its morning inspection, Bonnard said. From the caves in the cliffs came hundreds and hundreds of golden fliers, as if called inexorably by the thin thread of sunlight. Bonnard quickly aimed the recorder and caught the spectacle of hundreds of giffs, wings raised, beaks open, carolling a curious warble as they turned in the sparse sunlight.

'Ever seen anything like that before, Varian?' asked Kai in amazement.

'Not quite like that. Oh, they are beautiful creatures. Quick, Bonnard, on the third terrace to the left, get that lot!'

The giffs, one after the other, dropped off the ledge, wings spreading and lifting, soaring, turning over, as if letting each part of their bodies bathe in the sunlight. It was a slow aerial dance that held the observers spellbound.

'They've got their eyes closed,' Bonnard said, peering

through the focusing lens of the recorder. 'Hope they know where they're going.'

'They probably have some sort of radar perception,' said Varian. She increased her face-mask's magnification to observe more closely. 'I wonder . . . are their eyes closed for some mystical reason? Or simply because the sun is strong?'

'Carotene is good for your eyes,' said Bonnard.

Varian tried to recall if she'd ever seen a fang-face or one of the herbivores squint or close their eyes completely during sunshine. She couldn't remember. Full sunlight was a rare enough occasion so that all human eyes were invariably on the sun. She'd check the tapes out when she got back to the camp.

'Now, look Varian, only some of 'em are doing the flying act,' said Bonnard. He had swung around, recorder still operating, and focused on the juvenile giffs scratching about on the fish summit.

One of them let out a squawk, tried to back away from something and, overbalancing, fell back. Its companions regarded it for a long moment as it lay, flapping helplessly.

Without thinking, Varian began to climb towards the summit to assist the creature. She had put her hand over the top, when an adult giff, with a cry shrill enough to be a command, landed on the summit, awkwardly turning towards Varian. When she judiciously halted her climbing, the giff deftly flipped the juvenile to its feet with the wing claws. The wing remained a protective envelope above the young giff.

'Okay, I get the message, loud and clear,' said Varian.

A second grating sound issued from the adult giff whose eyes never left Varian.

'Varian!' Kai's call was warning and command.

'I'm all right. I've just been told to keep my distance.'

'Make it more distance, Varian. I'm covering you.'

'It would have attacked me if it was going to, Kai. Don't show the stunner.'

'How would they know what a stunner is?' asked Bonnard.

'Point! I'm going to offer the grass.' And slowly Varian

took the rift grasses from her leg pouch and with great care held up the sheaf for the giff to see.

The creature's eyes did not leave hers but Varian sensed that the grass had been noticed. She moved her hand slowly, to place the sheaf on the top of the summit. The giff made another grating noise, softer, less aggressive in tone.

'You're very welcome,' said Varian, and heard Bonnard's snort of disgust. 'Courtesy is never wasted, Bonnard. Tone conveys its own message. So does gesture. This creature understands a certain amount from both what I'm doing and what I'm saying.'

She had begun to descend to the sled's terrace level now, moving deliberately and never taking her eyes from the giff. As soon as she was back, standing with Kai and Bonnard, the adult giff waddled forward, took up the grass and then, returning to the sea-edge, dropped off. Once it had sufficient wing room, it soared up again and out of sight among the other fliers.

'That was fascinating,' said Kai on the end of a long held sigh.

Bonnard was regarding Varian with open respect.

'Wow! One poke of that beak and you'd've been sent over the edge.'

'There was no menace in the giff's action.'

'Varian,' said Kai, laying a hand on her arm, 'do be careful.'

'Kai, this isn't my first contact.' Then she saw the worry in his eyes. 'I am always careful. Or I wouldn't be here now. Making friends with alien creatures is my business. But how I'm ever to find out how mature their young are if they're this protective . . .' She stopped, whistled her surprise. 'I know. The giff was protective because it's used to protecting the juveniles. So, they're not equipped to protect themselves at birth, or for some time thereafter. Still,' and she sighed her disappointment, 'I would have liked to get inside one of their caves . . .'

'Look, Varian,' said Bonnard in a whisper and indicated the direction with the barest movement of his forefinger.

Slowly, Varian turned to see a row of juvenile giffs watching from the summit, wings in a closed position, tilted up beyond their backs, wing claws acting as additional supports to their sitting. Varian began to laugh, shaking her head and muttering about the observer observed.

'So we're fair peek,' said Kai, leaning against the edge of the sled and folding his arms. 'Now what do we do in your programme? Be observed in our daily morning habits?'

'You can, if you wish. Be interesting to see how long their attention span is, but there's a great deal going on up there.' She pointed skywards where the giffs were circling, but some groups spun off in various directions, with purposeful sweeps of their wings. 'We don't seem to have hit a day of rest,' she said, flashing a smile at Kai. 'Bonnard, if I give you a leg up on the sled's canopy, I think you can see the summit. Can you tell me what the juveniles were squawking about? Or what overbalanced the one I wanted to rescue?'

'Sure.'

'Just don't dance about too much. Your boots'll scar the plascreen. And no, you can't take 'em off,' Kai added as Bonnard began to speak.

They hoisted him up and, moving with great care, Bonnard positioned himself where he could see the summit.

'There's dead fringes up here, Varian, and some slimy looking seaweed. Aw, would you look at that?'

The juveniles, attracted by his new position, had abandoned that section of the summit and waddled over to stand directly in Bonnard's line of sight. Disgusted, he propped both hands against his hips and glared, actions which set them all to squawking and shifting away from the edge. Kai and Varian chuckled over the two sets of young.

'Hey, recorder man, you missed a dilly of a sequence!'

'Don't I just know it!'

'C'mon down,' Varian told him, having learned what she needed to know.

She wandered over to the sea edge of the terrace, lay down, peering further over the drop.

'I'm not allowed up. Am I allowed down? There appears to

be a cave over to the left, about twenty metres, Kai. If I use a belt-harness, you could probably swing me to it.'

Kai was not completely in favour of such gymnastics but the belt-harness, winched safely to the sled's exterior attachments, could hold a heavy-worlder securely. He was glad not to be at the end of the pendulum swing as she was to reach her objective.

'Are they watching, Bonnard?' Varian asked over the comunit.

'The young ones are, Varian, and yes, one of the airborne fliers is watching.'·

'Let's see if they have any prohibitive spots . . .'

'Varian . . .' Kai grew apprehensive as he, too, saw the adult giff fly in for a close look at Varian's swinging body.

'It's only looking, Kai. I expect that. One more swing now and . . . I got it.' She had grabbed and caught a stony protrusion at the cave entrance and agilely scrambled in.

'Rakers! It's abandoned. It's gigantic. Goes so far back I can't see the end.' Her voice over the comunit sounded muffled and then hollow.

'No, wait. Just what I wanted. An egg. An egg? And they let me in. Oh, it rattles. Dead egg. Small, too. Well, only circumstantial evidence that their young are born immature. Hmmm. There're grasses here, sort of forming a nest. Too scattered at this point to be sure. They can't have abandoned a cave because there's an infertile egg? No fish bones, or scales. They must devour whole. Good digestions then.'

Bonnard and Kai exchanged glances over her monologue and the assorted sounds of her investigations, broadcast from the comunit.

'The nest grasses are not the rift valley type, more like the tougher fibres of the swamp growths. I wonder . . . Okay, Kai,' and her broadcast voice was augmented by the clearer tones that indicated she had left the cave, 'pull me up.'

She had grasses sprouting from her leg pouches as she came over the lip of the ledge, and the egg made an unusual bulge in the front of her ship suit.

'Any sign of alarm?' she asked.

126

Kai, securing the winch, shook his head as Bonnard leaped to assist her out of the harness.

'Hey, their eggs are small. Can I shake it?'

'Go ahead. What's in it is long dead.'

'Why?'

Varian shrugged. 'We'll let Trizein have a gawk and see if he can find out. I don't necessarily wish to fracture it. Let me have that plascovering, Kai,' and she neatly stored the egg, surrounded by the dead grasses and then brushed her gloved hands together to signify a task well completed. 'That's thirsty work,' she said and led the way back to the sled where she broke out more rations.

'You know,' she said, half-way through the quick meal, 'I think that each of those groups was out on various set tasks . . .'

'So we're staying around to see what they bring home?' asked Kai.

'If you don't mind?'

'No.' He inclined his head towards the juveniles, some of whom had indeed lost interest and were bumbling about the summit at the far side. 'I'm enjoying the reversal of roles.'

'I wish I could get into a cave currently in use . . .'

'All in one day?'

'Yes, you're right, Kai. That's asking too much. At least, we've experienced no aggressive action from them. The adult construed my action as helpful rather than dangerous. It did accept the grass . . .'

They all glanced upward as an unusual note penetrated the sled's roof, a high pitched, sharp sustained note. The juveniles on the summit came rigidly to attention. Varian gestured to Bonnard to take the recorder but the boy was already reaching for it, doing a scan of the skies before he steadied the device on the alert young.

A mass of fliers fell from the caves, gained wing room and flew with an astonishing show of speed off into the misty south west.

'That's the direction of the sea gap. The net fishers?'

'The juveniles are clearing away,' said Bonnard. 'Looks like fish for lunch to me.'

Out of the mist now appeared wing-weary giffs, barely skimming the water, rising with obvious effort to ledges where they settled, wings unclosed and drooping. Varian was certain she'd seen grass trailing from the rear claws of one. They waited, and so did the juveniles, occasionally poking at each other. Bonnard, fretting with the interval, moved towards the sled exit but Varian stopped him, just as they saw an adult giff land on their terrace.

'Don't move a muscle, Bonnard.'

The adult watched, its eyes never moving from the sled.

'Now move slowly back from the exit,' Varian told him and when he had completed the manoeuvre, she let out a deep sigh of relief. 'What did I tell you the other day? You don't bother animals with their food. You sure as rakers don't bother creatures waiting for lunch, if you want to stay in good with them.'

'I'm sorry, Varian.'

'That's all right, Bonnard. You have to learn these things. Fortunately no harm's done – either to you or to our mission.' She smiled at Bonnard's downcast face. 'Cheer up. We've also learned something else. They haven't let up surveillance of *us* for one minute. And they've figured out where we enter and leave this sled. Pretty clever creatures, I'd say.'

Never taking his eyes off their guard, the boy sank to the floor of the sled.

They waited another three-quarters of an hour before Kai, remembering to keep his gesture slow, alerted them to the returning giffs. Cries raised from every quarter and so many giffs were airborne that Bonnard complained that his frames would show more furred bodies and wings than anything informative.

Bonnard and Varian saw a repetition of the previous performance as the shimmering piles of fish were spewed from the nets. The juveniles waddled in and one adult, spotting a youngster stocking up his throat pouch, tapped it smartly on the head and made it regurgitate. Kai observed another adult separating fringes from the mass, dextrously flipping them over the edge of the cliff with smart sweeps of his beak. When it had apparently completed that task on its side of the catch, it carefully scrubbed its beak against stone.

'I got that on tape, Varian,' Bonnard assured her as Kai pointed out another curiosity, an adult giff whose beak was being stuffed by others. The giff then waddled off the cliff edge, gained wing room and disappeared into one of the larger caves. Another took his place, to be filled up before flying off, this time to another large aperture. The juveniles were allowed to eat one fish at a time. There was a repeat of juvenile terror over a fringe, two fell over and were intertwined until rescued by a watching adult. Bonnard fretted at having to remain inside the sled instead of on it where he could have got much better tapes of the incident.

Gradually the supply dwindled, the juveniles losing interest and disappearing from the summit. Soon after, Varian noticed that no giffs were to be seen. They waited patiently until Kai became so restless with inactivity that Varian could not ignore the fact that they were not furthering their study of the giff by remaining either in the sled or on the terrace.

It was well past midday now. She'd enough on tapes for hours of study. Her announcement that they'd better get back to the compound met with instant action on the part of the two males. Kai checked the sled's lock for flight, motioned Bonnard to strap himself in and did so himself. Both were ready while she, laughing, was barely seated.

As she took off, she circled once more over the summit, noting that small fringes were left to bake and deteriorate on the summit. She'd answered a few of her questions, but more had been raised by the day's happenings. She was reasonably pleased with the excursion, if only because it had been something she'd wanted to do.

CHAPTER EIGHT

Kai noticed the absence of the sleds as they circled an encampment strangely motionless. Only Dandy was visible, half asleep in his pen, one hind leg cocked at the ankle. For some reason, that reassured Kai. Dandy had shown a marked tendency to react to any tension or excitement in the compound by cowering against the fencing of his pen.

'Everyone is indeed resting,' said Varian who was piloting the sled.

'My teams must have made an early return to their camps.'

'Yes, but where are my heavy-worlders? Not all the sleds should be gone.'

'Bakkun said something about going to his place,' said Bonnard.

'His place?' Kai and Varian asked in chorus.

'Yes. North,' said Bonnard, pointing. 'Bakkun's special place is in the north.'

'What sort of special place?' asked Varian, signalling Kai with a quick glance to let her do the questioning. 'Have you been there?'

'Yes, last week when I was out with Bakkun. It's not what I'd call special, just a clear circular place among the trees, closed off at one end by a rock fall. There's a bunch of the big grass-eaters, like Mabel, and some other smaller types. They've all got hunks out of their sides, Varian. Bakkun told me Paskutti was interested in them. Didn't he mention it to you?'

'Probably hasn't had time,' said Varian in such an off-handed manner that Kai knew Paskutti hadn't mentioned it to her.

'Time? That was a week ago.'

'We've all been busy,' said Varian, frowning as she slipped the sled into hold and landed it lightly on the ground.

Lunzie was at the veil lock now, waiting to open it for them.

'Successful trip?' she asked.

'Yes, indeed. Everyone enjoying a quiet restful day here, too?' asked Varian.

Lunzie gave her a long searching look.

'As far as I know,' said Lunzie slowly, her eyes never leaving Varian's as she closed the veil lock. 'Terilla's working on some drawings in Gaber's dome, and Cleiti's reading in the main dome.'

'Could I show Cleiti the tapes, Varian?'

'By all means. Just don't erase 'em by mistake!'

'Varian! I've been handling tapes for weeks with no blanking.'

Kai could sense that Varian wanted Bonnard out of earshot. He was also aware that somehow or other the two women had exchanged some tacit information and were impatient to talk uninhibitedly. Kai had a few questions to put to Varian, too, about Bakkun, Paskutti and trapped herbivores.

'My teams get off all right?' Kai asked Lunzie to cover the conspicuous silence as Bonnard made his way across the compound. He paused to pat Dandy.

'Yes, all except Bakkun, who went off with the heavy-worlders on some jaunt of their own.' Lunzie gestured towards the shuttle and they moved that way. 'Remember asking me about the stores, Kai?' she said in a low voice. 'Someone raided our hold of a selection of basic medical supplies. Also, the synthesizer has been used enough to drain a power pack. Now the synthesizer may be heavy on power but *I* hadn't used it that much on the new pack. So I had Portegin check it out this morning before he went off, and there's no malfunction. Someone's been using it. What was synthesized I couldn't say.'

'Where did the heavy-worlders go, Lunzie?' Varian asked.

'I don't know. I was in the stores by then, when I heard sled and belts going. Then Portegin came, told me the heavy-worlders had taken off . . .' Lunzie paused, frowning in concentration 'That's odd. I was in the store hold, and they didn't come to me for any rations.'

'No!' Varian's low exclamation startled the doctor and Kai.

'What's wrong, Varian?'

She had turned very pale, looked suddenly quite sick and leaned against the bulkhead.

'No, I must be wrong.'

'Wrong?' Lunzie prompted her.

'I must be. There'd be no reason for them to revert. Would there, Lunzie?'

'Revert?' Lunzie stared intently at Varian who was still leaning weakly against the bulkhead. 'You can't think . . .'

'Why else would Paskutti be interested in flank-wounded herbivores that I didn't know anything about? I never thought Bakkun was callous. But, to say such a thing in front of a boy . . .'

Lunzie gave a snort. 'The heavy-worlders don't have a high opinion of adult light gravs, less of the ship-bred, and children on their worlds never speak until they've killed . . .'

'What are you two talking about?' asked Kai.

'I'm afraid I agree with Varian's hypothesis.'

'Which is?' Kai spoke testily.

'That the heavy-worlders have taken to eating animal protein.' Lunzie's calm detached tone did not lessen the impact of such a revolting statement.

Kai thought he would be ill, the sudden nausea was so acute.

'They've . . .' He couldn't repeat the sentence and waived one hand in lieu of the words. 'They're Federation members. They're civilized . . .'

'They do conform when in Federation company,' said Varian in a low colourless voice, indicating how deeply shocked she was. 'But I've worked with them in expeditions before and they will . . . if they can. I just didn't think . . . I didn't want to think they'd do it here.'

'They have been discreet,' said Lunzie. 'Not that I'm defending them. If it hadn't been for Bonnard's chance remark . . . No,' and Lunzie frowned at the floor plates, 'I've been skirting the edges of a theory ever since that night . . .'

'The night you served them the fruit distillation.' Varian rounded on Lunzie, pointing at her. 'They weren't drunk!

132

They were high. And you know why?' Neither had time to answer her hypothetical question. 'Because of the violence . . .'

'Yes, violence and alcohol would act as stimuli on the heavy-worlders,' said Lunzie, nodding her head judiciously. 'They have a naturally slow metabolism,' she told Kai. 'And a low sex drive which makes them an admirable mutation for EEC expeditions. Given the proper stimulants and . . .' Lunzie shrugged.

'That's my fault. I shouldn't have let them drink that night. I knew. You see,' Varian rushed on in a spate of confession, 'that was the day a fang-face savagely attacked a herbivore. I noticed Paskutti and Tardma reacting strongly although I *thought* at the time I was imagining things . . .'

'That was the violence needed and I compounded the problem by offering the fruit distillation.' Lunzie was willing to share the responsibility. 'They must have made quite a night of it.'

'And we thought they'd gone to bed early!' Varian clapped her palm on her forehead, admitting stupidity. 'With too potent a brew . . .' She started to laugh and then, drew in her breath sharply, 'Oh, no!'

'Now what?' demanded Kai sharply.

'They went back.'

'Went back?' Kai was confused.

'Remember my asking you about the big sled's flight time?' Varian asked Kai.

'They went back and slaughtered that herbivore for its flesh?' Lunzie asked Varian.

'I wish you didn't need to be so revoltingly vulgar,' said Kai, angry at the doctor as well as himself and his churning stomach.

'Yes,' Lunzie continued, ignoring Kai, 'they would definitely need additional animal protein . . .'

'Lunzie!' Now Varian tried to stop her but the physician continued in her detached clinical way.

'I do believe they eat, and enjoy, animal protein. On their own planet, they have to eat it, little vegetable matter grows on high grav worlds that is digestible by human stock. Gener-

133

ally they will conform to the universal standards of vegetable and synthetic proteins. I have given them subsistence foods high in . . .' Lunzie stopped 'Could that be why the synthesizer was overworked?'

'Protein?' asked Kai, desperately hoping that members of his expedition had not abrogated all the tenets of acceptable dietary controls.

'No, the other daily requirements they couldn't get from a purely animal diet. One thing that isn't missing from our stores is our sort of protein.'

Varian, looking green, held up a hand to divert Lunzie.

'Didn't think you were the squeamish type, Varian,' Lunzie said. 'Still, your sensitivity does credit to your upbringing. The temptation to eat animal flesh is still strong in the planet-bred . . .'

'Kai, what are we going to do?' asked Varian.

'Frankly,' said Lunzie, 'though you didn't ask me, I'd say there was nothing you can do. They have been discreet about their vile preference. However,' and her tone altered, 'this only supports my contention that you can never successfully condition away a basic urge. It requires generations in a new environment to be positive of your results. Oh!' Lunzie had begun in her usual confident, pedantic tone. Her exclamation was startled. 'I say, Kai, Varian,' she looked from one to the other at her most solemn, 'EV *is* returning for us, isn't it?'

'We have every reason to believe so,' said Kai firmly.

'Why do you ask, Lunzie?' Again Varian seemed to hear something in the woman's question that Kai had missed.

'Gaber doesn't believe so.'

'As I told Dimenon,' said Kai, feeling the need to show unconcerned authority, 'we are out of contact but if the Theks aren't worried, neither am I.'

'The Theks never worry,' said Lunzie. 'Worry is for people pressed by time. How long have we been out of contact, Kai?'

He hesitated only long enough to catch Varian's eye and her approval. Lunzie was a good ally.

'Since the first reports were stripped from the satellite.'

'That long?'

'We surmise, and the Theks confirm it, that the cosmic storm EV was going to investigate after leaving us, has caused interference and EV can't reach the satellite.'

Lunzie nodded, stroking the back of her neck as if her muscles were taut.

'I gather Gaber has been spouting that asinine theory of his, that we're planted?' Kai managed a laugh that sounded, to him, genuinely amused.

'I laughed at Gaber, too, but I don't think the heavy-worlders have the same sense of humour.'

'That would account for their aggressive behaviour,' said Varian. 'They'd be very much at home on this planet, and strong enough to survive.'

'This generation would be strong enough,' said Lunzie in her pedantic tone, 'but not the next.'

'What are you talking like that for?' Kai demanded angrily. '"Next generation". We aren't planted!'

'No, I don't think *we* are,' and Lunzie was calm. 'We're much too small a group for a genetic pool and the wrong ages. But that wouldn't inhibit the heavy-worlders from striking out . . .'

'Staying on Ireta?' Kai was appalled.

'Oh, they've everything here they require,' said Lunzie. 'Alcohol, animal protein . . . The heavy-worlders are often laws unto themselves. You've heard the tales, Varian,' and the girl nodded slowly. 'I've heard of several groups just fading into the scenery. If you can imagine the bulk of a heavy-worlder fading . . .'

'They can't do that,' Kai said, wrestling with dismay, anger and a sense of futility for he hadn't a notion how to prevent the heavy-worlders from carrying out such a plan. Physically they were superior, and both he and Varian had often felt that the heavy-worlders merely tolerated them as leaders because it suited.

'They could, and we had better admit it to ourselves, if to no one else,' said Lunzie. 'Unless, of course, you can figure out something so disastrous about this planet that they'd

135

prefer to return with us.' It was obvious she felt that there could be no such circumstance to deter the heavy-worlders.

'Now, there's a constructive thought,' said Varian.

'Retro, please,' said Kai. 'We have no indication that that is their intention! We may have just talked ourselves into a crisis without any substantiation. Muhlah! It's no business of ours to interfere with the sexual requirements of any group. If they have to have stimuli to satisfy their drive, fine. We've created the indiscretion by ascribing unsavoury and unacceptable actions to them and we don't even know if our speculations are valid.'

Lunzie looked a little chagrined but Varian was not so easily mollified.

'I don't like it! Something's out of phase. I've felt it since the day we went to Mabel's assistance.'

'Violence is a stimulus for the heavy-worlders,' said Lunzie. 'And despite our strides towards true civilized behaviour, it can prove a stimulus for us as well: a primitive, disgusting but valid reaction.' Lunzie shrugged her acceptance of such frailty. 'We aren't that far removed from the slime of creation and instinctive response ourselves. From now on, I shall judiciously dilute the distillation for everyone.' She walked towards the exit. 'And no one will be the wiser.'

'Look, Varian, we don't *know* yet,' said Kai, seeing how dejected Varian was. 'We've taken isolated facts—'

'*I've* taken isolated facts . . . but Kai, something *is* wrong.'

'—Too much already. We don't need more.'

'Leaders are supposed to anticipate problems so that they don't arise.'

'Like EV failing to contact us?' Kai gave her a long amused look.

'That's EV's problem, not ours. Kai, I've worked with heavy-worlders before. I even . . .' she gave a weak laugh, 'survived two weeks of gravity on Thormeka to have some understanding of the conditions that bred them. And I *did* notice that Paskutti and Tardma overreacted to fang-face's attack on the herbivore. As much as heavy-worlders do react.'

'We cannot interfere with the discreet sexual practices of

any group, Varian, can we?' He waited until she'd reluctantly agreed. 'So, we've now anticipated that there might be a problem, right?'

'It's my first big expedition, Kai. It's got to turn out right.'

'My dear co-leader, you've been doing a superior job.' Kai pulled her from the bulkhead and into his arms. He didn't like to see the volatile Varian so dejected and, he sincerely hoped, needlessly worried. 'None of my geology teams have been trampled or flank bitten . . . You've sorted out some new life forms, a bonus on *your* binary bit, my friend. And you know, it'd be nice if we practised some sex ourselves?'

He startled her and laughed at her reaction, took her silence as acquiescence and kissed her. Meeting with no resistance and some co-operation, they retired, discreetly, to his dome for the remainder of the rest day.

CHAPTER NINE

A world which stimulated last evening's occupation couldn't be all bad, Varian decided the next morning, rising totally refreshed. Perhaps Lunzie had been wrong to think that just because the heavy-worlders hadn't taken along protein rations, they were going to . . . Well, there was no proof that their day hadn't been spent in gratifying their sex drive, and not an atavistic pleasure in dietary habits.

Kai was correct, too. As they had no proof of any misdemeanour, it did no good to harbour base suspicions.

Easier said than done, thought Varian later as she conferred with the heavy-worlders on the week's assignments. She could not put her finger on a specific change, but there was a marked difference in the attitude of her team. Varian had always felt relatively at ease with Paskutti and Tardma. Today, she was conscious of a restraint, stumbling for phrases and words, uncomfortable and feeling that Paskutti and Tardma were amused by her. They had an air of smug satisfaction that irritated her, though she'd be hard pressed to say what gave her that idea as the heavy-worlders betrayed no emotion. The xenob team was keeping just ahead of the areas the geologists must probe on the ground. Unknown life forms lurked in the heavy vegetation, small but equally dangerous, and force-screen belts were not absolute protection.

As the two heavy-worlders strode beside her towards the sled park, she could have sworn that Paskutti was limping slightly. Varian and Kai had agreed to hold off questioning the heavy-worlders and Varian had no trouble controlling her curiosity that day. That indefinable change in the heavy-worlders' attitude towards her acted as a crucial check.

It was a distinct relief to her to call an end to the day's scouting when pelting, wind-lashed rain limited visibility and made telltagging impossible. That it was Paskutti who called the actual halt to the exercise gave Varian some measure of satisfaction.

When they entered the compound, Lunzie was crossing from the shuttle to her quarters and gave Varian an imperceptible signal to join her.

'Something occurred yesterday,' the physician told Varian in the privacy. 'Tanegli has a gash across one cheek-bone. He said he got it from a sharp twig when leaning over to collect a specimen.' Lunzie's expression discounted that explanation. 'And I'm certain that Paskutti is masking a limp.'

'Oho, and Bakkun is not making full use of his left arm.'

'In some primitive societies, the males fight for the favour of the females,' Varian said.

'That doesn't hold. Berru is wearing heal-seal on her left arm. I haven't seen Divisti or the others today, but I'd love to call a medical on all of 'em. Only I did that too recently for the alcohol reaction.'

'Maybe Berru just didn't like the male who won her?'

Lunzie snorted. 'I'd say the air was blue with response yesterday. Anyway, how come you're in so early?'

'Violent storm, couldn't see, and certainly couldn't tell tag what was on the ground. I rather thought though,' she added in a drawl, 'that Paskutti and Tardma were quite ready to quit early.'

'I've put a new power pack in the synthesizer and I'll keep strict account of my usage. Tanegli says he found two more edible fruits, and one plant heart with a high nutritional content. At least he *says* he found them yesterday . . .'

'We could still be computing from the wrong data,' suggested Varian wistfully.

'We could be.' Lunzie was not convinced.

'I could ask Bonnard if he remembers the co-ordinates of Bakkun's so-called special place?'

'You could, though I *don't* like involving the youngsters in any part of this.'

'Nor do I. But they are part of the expedition and this could affect them as well as us adults. However, I could just be in the general vicinity of Bakkun's run that day, and . . .'

'Yes, that would not be a blatant abuse of the child's trust.'

'I'll see what Kai says.'

Kai had the same general objection to involving the youngster at all. On the other hand, it was important to find out exactly what had occurred, and if the heavy-worlders were reverting, he and Varian would have to know and take steps. He cautioned Varian to be discreet, both with Bonnard and the search.

Her opportunity came about quite naturally two mornings later. Kai and Bonnard took off north to do a depth assessment of a pitchblende strike discovered by Berru and Triv. Paskutti and Tardma followed by lift-belt to track and tag some shallow water monsters observed, at a safe distance, by the two geologists. Varian wanted to penetrate and telltag further to the north west so she asked Bonnard to be her team flyer.

She did a good deal of work with Bonnard and managed casually to veer to the proper heading. She had checked Bakkun's flight tapes.

'Say, isn't this near where Bakkun had those herbivores?'

Turning from the telltagger, Bonnard glanced around.

'A lot of Ireta looks the same, purple-green trees and no sun. No, wait. That line of fold mountains, with the three higher overthrusts . . .'

'You have learned a thing or two,' said Varian, teasingly.

Bonnard faltered, embarrassed. 'Well, Bakkun's been giving me instruction, you know. We were headed straight for that central peak, I think. And we landed just above the first fold of those hills.' Then he added, 'We found some gold there, you know.'

'Gold's the least of the riches this planet holds.'

'Then we're not likely to be left, are we?'

Varian inadvertently swerved, sending Bonnard against his seat straps. She corrected her course, cursing Gaber's big mouth and her own lack of self-control.

'Gaber's wishful thinking, huh?' she asked, hoping her chuckle sounded amused. 'Those old fogeys get like that, wanting to extend their last expeditionary assignment as long as they can.'

'Oh.' Bonnard had not considered that possibility. 'Terilla told me he sounded awful certain.'

'Wishful thinking often does sound like fact. Say, you don't want to stay on Ireta, too, do you? Thought you didn't like this stinking planet, Bonnard?'

'It's not so bad, once you get used to the smell.'

'Just don't get too accustomed, pal. We've got to go back to the EV. Now, keep your eyes open, I want to check . . .'

They were flying over the first of the hills but Varian didn't need Bonnard to tell her when they cruised over Bakkun's special place. It was clearly identifiable: some of the heavier bones and five skulls still remained. Stunned and unwillingly committed now, Varian circled the sled to land and also saw the heavy, blackened stones, witness to a campfire which the intervening days' rain had not quite washed away.

She said nothing. She was grateful that Bonnard couldn't and wouldn't comment.

She put the sled down between the fire site and the first of the skulls. It was pierced between the eyes with a round hole: too large to have been a stun bolt at close range, but whatever had driven it into the beast's head had had enough force behind it to send fracture lines along the skull bone. Two more skulls showed these holes, the fourth had been crushed by heavy blows on the thinner base of the neck. The fifth skull was undamaged and it was not apparent how that creature had met its death.

The ground in the small rock-girded field was torn up and muddied with tracks, giving silent evidence to struggles.

'Varian,' Bonnard's apologetic voice called her from chaotic speculations. He was holding up a thin scrap of fabric, stiff and darker than ship suits should be, a piece of sleeve fabric for the seam ran to a bit of the tighter cuff: a big cuff, a left arm cuff. She winced with revulsion but shoved the offending evidence into her thigh pocket.

Resolutely she strode to the makeshift fire-pit, staring at the blackened stones, at the groove chipped out of opposing stones where a spit must have been placed. She shuddered against rising nausea.

'We've seen enough, Bonnard,' she said, gesturing him to follow her back to the sled. She had all she could do not to run from the place.

When they had belted into their seats, she turned to Bonnard, wondering if her face was as white as his.

'You will say nothing of this to anyone, Bonnard. Nothing.'

Her fingers trembled as she made a note of the co-ordinates. When she lifted the sled, she shoved in a burst of propulsion, overwhelmingly eager to put as much space between her and that charnel spot as she could!

Neither she nor Kai could ignore such an abrogation of basic Federation tenets. For a fleeting moment, she wished she'd made this search alone, then she could have forgotten about it, or tried to. With Bonnard as witness, the matter could not be put aside as a nightmare. The heavy-worlders would have to be officially reprimanded, though she wasn't sure how efficacious words would be against their physical strength. They were contemptuous enough of their leadership already to have killed and eaten animal flesh.

Varian shook her head sharply, trying to clear her mind of the revulsion that inevitably accompanied that hideous thought.

'Life form, untagged,' Bonnard said in a subdued tone.

Willing for any diversion from her morbid and sickening thoughts, Varian turned the sled, tracking the creature until it crossed a clearing.

'Got it,' said Bonnard. 'It's a fang-face, Varian. And Varian, it's wounded. Rakers!'

The predator whirled in the clearing, reaching up to beat futilely at the air with its short fore-feet. A thick branch had apparently lodged in its ribs, Varian could see fresh blood from its exertions flowing out of the gaping wound. Then she could no longer ignore the fact that the branch was a crude spear, obviously flung with great force into the beast's side.

'Aren't we going to try and help it, Varian?' asked Bonnard as she sent the sled careering away.

'We couldn't manage it alone, Bonnard.'

'But it will die.'

'Yes, and there's nothing we can do now. Not even get close enough to spray a seal on the wound and hope that it could dislodge that . . .' She didn't know why she stopped; she wasn't protecting the heavy-worlders, and Bonnard had seen the horror.

Hadn't the carnivores provided the heavy-worlders with enough violence? How many other wounded creatures would she and Bonnard encounter in this part of the world?

'By any chance, had you the taper on, Bonnard?'

'Yes, I did, Varian.'

'Thank you. I'm turning back. I must speak to Kai as soon as possible.' When she saw Bonnard looking at the communit, she shook her head. 'This is an executive matter, Bonnard. Again, I must ask you to say nothing to anyone and . . .' She wanted to add 'stay away from the heavy-worlders' but from the tight, betrayed expression on the boy's face, she knew such advice would be superfluous.

They continued back to the compound in silence for a while.

'Varian?'

'Yes, Bonnard?' She hoped she had an answer for him.

'Why? Why did they do such a terrible thing?'

'I wish I knew, Bonnard. No incidence of violence stems from a *simple* cause, or a single motive. I've always been told that violence is generally the result of a series of frustrations and pressures that have no other possible outlet.'

'An action has a reaction, Varian. That's the first thing you learn shipboard.'

'Yes, because you're often in free-fall or outer space, so the first thing *you'd* have to learn, ship-bred, is to control yourself, your actions.'

'On a heavy world, though,' Bonnard was trying to rationalize so hard, Varian could almost hear him casting about for a justification. 'On a heavy world, you would have struggle all the time, against the gravity.'

'Until you became so used to it, you wouldn't consider it a struggle. You'd be conditioned to it.'

'Can you be conditioned to violence?' Bonnard sounded appalled.

Varian gave a bark of bitter laughter. 'Yes, Bonnard, you can be conditioned to violence. Millenniums ago, it used to be the general human condition.'

'I'm glad I'm alive now.'

To that Varian made no reply, wondering if she was in accord. In an earlier time, when people were still struggling to a civilized level that spurned the eating of animal flesh; to a level that had learned not to impose its peculiar standards on any other species; to a level that accepted, as a matter of course, the friendships and associations with beings diverse and wonderful: a woman of only three hundred years ago would have had some occasion to cope with utter barbarianism. It was one matter entirely for beasts to fight and kill each other, following the dictates of an ecology (not that she was prevented from succouring the weaker when she could), but for one species, stronger, more flexible, basically more dangerous because of its versatility, to attack a stupid animal for the sporting pleasure was unspeakably savage.

What were she and Kai to do about such behaviour? Again she wished she hadn't brought Bonnard. She'd been too clever, so she had, involving the boy. Perhaps scarring him with such evidence of wanton cruelty. But she hadn't expected anything like this when she thought of investigating Bakkun's special place. How could she? And once discovered, strong measures were indicated. Too late now to say that the heavy-worlders had been discreet in their vile pursuits. Too late to wish she'd never wanted to check into their activities.

On the other hand, such aberrant behaviour was better uncovered on a world where no other sentient species was compromised. She also found some measure of relief that the heavy-worlders had picked on the stupid herbivores and predators, rather than the lovely golden giffs. If they'd harmed them . . . Pure rage, such as she had never experienced before in her life, consumed her with an incredible force.

Startled, Varian composed her thoughts. She must discipline herself if she wanted to control others.

They were almost to the compound now, sweeping down the broad plain that led to their granite height. Varian found herself hoping that, for some unknown reaons, Kai had returned early. That was the trouble with bad news: it didn't keep. The intelligence was a sore weight in her mind, festering with speculation, such as what were the heavy-worlders doing right now?

She landed, reminding Bonnard to say nothing, even to Cleiti or Terilla, most certainly not to Gaber.

'You bet not Gaber,' said Bonnard with a smile. 'He talks an awful lot but he says so little . . . unless he's talking about maps and beamed shots.'

'Wait a minute, Bonnard.' Varian motioned him back, wondering about the wisdom of involving him further. She glanced towards the shimmering force-screen, the dance of dying insects registering blue across the field. She tried to think, calmly, whether there was anyone else in the compound she could trust. Then she glanced back at the boy, standing easily, his head slightly cocked as he awaited her command. 'Bonnard, I'm taking the power pack from this sled. When the other sleds come in, I want you to remove the packs – hide them in the underbrush if you can't bring them inside. If any one questions you, say that your chore is checking them for lead drains. Yes, that's logical. Do you understand me?' She was unclamping their sled's pack as she issued her instructions. 'You know where the packs are in the smaller sleds? And how to remove them?'

'Portegin showed us. Besides, I just saw you do it.' He gave her the hand-lift which she attached to the heavy power pack and heaved it from the sled. 'I'll just get another hand-lift.'

She could see in his expression that he had more questions he was eager to ask as he followed her to the veil lock where Lunzie now stood to admit them. As they passed her, the woman looked at the power pack Varian was trailing.

'One of the leads is clogged,' Varian said.

'Is that why you're back so early? Good thing,' and

145

Lunzie's usually solemn face broke into a wide grin. She gestured towards Dandy's pen. Trizein was leaning on the fencing, staring intently at the little creature who was, for a second marvel, peacefully munching at a pile of grasses, oblivious to the scrutiny.

'Trizein's out of his lab? What happened?'

'I'll let him tell you. It's his surprise, not mine.'

'Surprise?'

'Here, Bonnard, take the power pack from Varian and put it where it belongs . . .'

Varian indicated the shuttle to Bonnard, a gesture which brought a surprised glance from Lunzie.

'Well, then,' she said, 'in the shuttle and come straight back. You'll want to hear about the probable ancestry of your pet, too.'

'Huh?' Bonnard was startled.

'Quick, to the shuttle with the pack.' Lunzie shooed him off with both hands. 'The power pack leads, Varian? That's a bit lame, isn't it?'

'Varian! Has Lunzie told you?' Trizein had looked away from Dandy and seen her. 'Why didn't anyone tell me? I mean, I can speculate possibilities from disembodied tissues, but this . . . creature from our prehistoric past . . .'

His words were diversion enough but the ringing tone in which he spoke made Varian move more quickly to him.

'Prehistoric past? What do you mean, Trizean?'

'Why, this little specimen is an excellent example of a primitive herbivore . . .'

'I know that . . .'

'No, no, my dear Varian, not just *a* primitive herbivore of this planet, but an Earth-type herbivore, of the group perissodactyl.'

'Yes, I know it's perissodactyl. The axis of the foot is through the middle toe.'

'Varian, are you being dense on purpose to tease me? *This*,' and Trizein gestured dramatically to Dandy, 'is the first step in the genotype of the horse. He's a genuine hyracotherium, *Earth* type!'

146

The significance of Trizein's point gradually dawned on Varian.

'You're trying to tell me that this is not *similar* to an Earth-type horse, it *is* the lineal ancestor of an Earth-type horse?'

'That's exactly what I'm telling you. Not trying. Telling!'

'It isn't possible.' Varian said that flatly and her expression accused Trizein of teasing her.

Trizein chuckled, preening himself by straightening his shoulders as he beamed at each member of his small audience.

'I may seem to be the original absent-minded analytical chemist, but my conclusions are always provable: my experiments conducted efficiently and as expeditiously as equipment and circumstance allow. Lately I've been wondering if someone has been trying to fool me, to test my ability or my tendency to digress. I assure you that I do know when two totally different life forms are presented to me as co-existing on this planet. It is too bad of someone. And I inform you right now that I am aware of this subterfuge. All the tissues you and your teams have been giving me suggest a sufficient variety of creatures to populate several planets, not just one. Didn't the Ryxi bring their own technicians? Is there life on the Thek planet that I'm being given such diverse . . .'

'What about that animal tissue that Bakkun gave you about a week ago?' It was a chance but she wasn't surprised when Trizein answered her.

'Oh, yes, the cellular level is remarkably comparable. A vertebrate, of course, which checks to ten decimal places, mitotic spindle, mitochondria all quite ordinary in a haemoglobin based species. Like that fellow there!' And he jerked his thumb at Dandy. 'Ah, Bonnard,' he said as the boy approached them. 'I undertsand from Lunzie that you rescued the little fellow?'

'Yes, sir, I did. But what is he?'

'A hyracotherium, or I miss my guess,' said Trizein with the forced joviality an adult often displayed for the unknown quantity of a youngster.

'Does that make Dandy special?' asked Bonnard of Varian,

'If he is a genuine hyracotherium, unusually special,' said Varian in a strangled voice.

'You doubt me,' Trizein said, aggrieved. 'You doubt me! But I can prove it.' He grabbed Varian by the elbow and Lunzie by the shoulder and marched them towards the shuttle. 'One is not allowed to bring much of a personal nature on a small short term expedition such as this, but I did bring my own data discs. You'll see.'

As they were propelled into the shuttle, Varian knew what she would see. For all his erratic speech and mental mannerisms, Trizein was invariably accurate. She only wished his data discs would indicate how Dandy's species got to Ireta. It was no consolation either to realize that Trizein was likely to prove that the hot-blooded pentadactyls were aliens to this planet, and the fringes with their cell construction of filaments were native. It was all part of the total confusion of this expedition: planted or mislaid, exploring a planet already once cored, out of control with the mother ship and in danger of a mutiny.

Trizein had shoved them into his lab and was now rummaging in his carry-sack which swung from a bolt in the ceiling, withdrawing a carefully wrapped bundle of data storage discs. He located the one he wanted and, with an air of righteous triumph, inserted it into the terminal's slot. There was no indecision about the keys he tapped and, as he pressed the print-out tab, he turned towards them with an expectant look.

Before their eyes was a replica, except for colouration, of Dandy. Neatly printed, the legend read 'Hyracotherium, Terra-Olicogene Age. Extinct.' Where Bonnard's pet had mottled reddish-brown fur, this creature was more dun and stripe: the difference necessitated by camouflage requirements, Varian realized, from one environment to another. An indication, also, that the creature had evolved to some extent here on Ireta. His presence made no sense yet.

'I don't understand about Dandy being like this old Earth beast. He's extinct,' said Bonnard, turning questioningly to Varian. 'I thought you couldn't find duplicate life forms developing independently on spatially distant planets. And

Ireta isn't even the same sort of planet as Earth. The sun's third generation.'

'We have observed inconsistencies about Ireta,' said Lunzie in her dry comforting voice.

'Is there any question in your mind about this creature's similarity now?' asked Trizein, exceedingly pleased with his performance.

'None, Trizein. But you were out in the compound before, why didn't you notice Dandy's similarity then?'

'My dear, I was out in the compound?' Trizein affected dazed surprise.

'You were, but your mind was undoubtedly on more important matters,' said Lunzie, a bit sharply.

'Quite likely,' said Trizein with dignity. 'My time has been heavily scheduled with analyses and tests and all kinds of interruptions. I've had little time to look around this world, though I have, you might say, examined it intimately.'

'Do you have other extinct and ancient Earth-type animals on that disc as well as Dandy?'

'Dandy? Oh, the Hyracotherium? Yes, this is my Earth paleontological disc, I have ancient species from . . .'

'We'd better stick to one set of puzzles at a time, Trizein,' said Varian, not certain he could absorb more conundrums today. If the fringes should turn out to be a life form from Beta Camaridae, she'd go twisted. 'Bonnard, the tape on the giffs is in the main console, isn't it?'

'I put it on data retrieval hold when I showed it to Cleiti and Terilla. Under the date, and giffs, Varian.'

Varian tapped up the proper sequence on the terminal and also transferred Trizein's disc to the smaller screen and a hold. The terminal screen cleared to a vivid frame of a golden flier, its crested head tilted slightly, enhancing the impression of its intelligence.

'Great heavens above! And furred. Definitely furred,' cried Trizein, bending to peer intently at the giff. 'There has always been a great deal of controversy about that among my colleagues. No way to be certain, of course, but this is unquestionably a Pteranodon!'

'Pteranodon?' Bonnard squirmed, uncomfortable to hear such a ponderous name attached to a creature he liked.

'Yes, a Pteranodon, a form of dinosaur, misnamed, of course since patently this creature is warm-blooded . . . inhabiting ancient Earth in Mesozoic times. Died out before the Tertiary period began. No one knows why, though there are as many speculations about the cause . . .' Trizein suddenly warded off the face that flashed on the screen for Varian had tapped in another sequence from the data banks. The heavy jawed head of a fang-face snarled up at them. 'Varian! It's . . . it's Tyrannosaurus rex. My dear, what sort of a crude joke are you attempting to play on me?' He was furious.

'That is no joke,' said Lunzie, nodding solemnly.

Trizein stared at her, his eyes protruding from his skull as his jaw dropped. He glanced back at the predatory countenance of the tyrant lizard, a name which Varian thought extremely suited to its bearer.

'Those creatures are alive on this planet?'

'Very much so. Do you have this Tyrannosaurus rex on your data disc?'

Almost reluctantly, and with a finger that noticeably trembled, Trizein tapped out a sequence for his own disc. The mild features and small body of Hyracotherium was replaced by the upright haughty and dangerous form of fang-face's prototype. Again there was a difference in colouration.

'The force screen,' said Trizein, 'is it strong enough to keep *it* outside?'

Varian nodded. 'It should be. Furthermore, there aren't any of this kind within a comfortable ten to fifteen kilometres of us. When we moved in, they moved out. They have other, more docile game than us.' The shudder that rippled down her spine was not for fear of Tyrannosaurus rex.

'You're sure it will keep its distance?' asked Trizein, concerned. 'That creature *ruled* its millenniums on old Earth. Why, he was supreme. Nothing could defeat him.'

Varian recalled all too vividly a tree-branch of a spear inextricably lodged in a tyrant lizard's rib cage.

'He doesn't like sleds, Trizein,' said Bonnard, not noticing her silence. 'He runs from them.'

The chemist regarded the boy with considerable scepticism.

'He does,' Bonnard repeated. 'I've seen him. Only today . . .' Then he caught Varian's repressive glance but Trizein hadn't noticed.

The man sank slowly to the nearest lab bench.

'Varian might tease me, and so might the boy, but Lunzie . . .'

It was as if Trizein, too, wished to hear a negative that would reassure him, restore matters to a previous comfortable balance. Lunzie, shaking her head, confirmed that the creatures did exist, and others of considerable size and variety.

'Stegosaurus, too? And the thunder lizard, the original dinosaur? And . . .' Trizein was torn between perturbation and eager excitement at the thought of seeing alive creatures he had long considered extinct. 'Why was I never told about them? I should have been told! It's my specialty, my hobby, prehistorical life forms.' Now Trizein sounded plaintive and accusatory.

'Believe me, my friend, it was not a conscious omission,' said Lunzie, patting his hand.

'I'm the true xenob, Trizein,' asid Varian in apology. 'It never occurred to me that these weren't unique specimens. I've only started considering that an anomaly must exist when you analysed the fringe types and found them to be on such a different cellular level. That and the grasses!'

'The grasses? The grasses! And tissue slides and blood plates, and all the time,' now outrage stirred Trizein to his feet, 'all the time these fantastic creatures are right . . . right outside the force screen. It's too much! Too much, and no one would tell me!'

'You were outside the compound, Trizein, oh you who look and do not see,' said Lunzie.

'If you hadn't kept me so busy with work, each of you saying it was vital and important, and had top priority. Never have I had to deal so single-handedly with so many top priorities, animal, vegetable and mineral. How I've kept going . . .'

'Truly, we're sorry, Trizein. More than you know. I wish I had pried you out of the lab much earlier,' said Varian so emphatically that Trizein was mollified. 'On more counts than identifying the beasts.'

Nevertheless, would that knowledge and identification have kept the heavy-worlders from their bestial game? Would it matter in the final outcome, Varian wondered.

'Well, well, make up for your omissions now. Surely this isn't all you have?'

Grateful for any legitimate excuse to delay the unpleasant, Varian gestured Trizein to be seated on something more comfortable than a bench and tapped out a sequence for her survey tapes, compiled when she and Terilla were doing the charts.

'It is patently obvious,' said the chemist, when he had seen all the species she had so far taped and tagged, 'that someone has played a joke. Not necessarily on me, on you, or us,' he added, glancing about from under his heavy brows. 'Those animals were planted here.'

Bonnard gargled an exclamation, not as controlled in his reaction to that phrase as Lunzie or Varian.

'Planted?' Varian managed a wealth of amused disbelief in that laughed word.

'Well, certainly they didn't spring up in an independent evolution, my dear Varian. They must have been brought here . . . '

'Fang-face, and herbivores and the golden fliers? Oh, Trizein, it isn't possible. Besides which the difference in pigmentation indicates that they *evolved* here . . . '

'Oh yes, but they *started* on Earth. I don't consider camouflage or pigmentation a real deterrant to my theory. All you'd need is one common ancestor. Climate, food, terrain would all bring about specialization over the millenniums and the variety of types would evolve. (The big herbivores, for instance, undoubtedly developed from Struthiomimus but so did Tyrannosaurus and, quite possibly, your Pteranodon.) The

152

possibilities are infinite from one mutual ancestor. Look at humans, for instance, in our infinite variations.'

'I'll grant it's possible, Trizein, but why? Who would do such a crazy thing? For what purpose? Why perpetuate such monstrosities as fang-face? I could see the golden fliers . . .'

'My dear, variety is essential in an ecological balance. And the dinosaurs were marvellous creatures. They ruled old Earth for more millenniums than we poor badly engineered *homo sapiens* have existed as a species. Who knows why they faded? What catastrophe occurred . . . More than likely a radical change in temperature following a magnetic shift – that's my theory at any rate, and I'll support it with the evidence we've found here. Oh, I do think this is a splendid development. A planet that has remained in the Mesozoic condition for untold millions of years, and is likely to remain so for unknown millenniums longer. The thermal core, of course, is the factor that . . .'

'Who, Trizein, rescued the dinosaurs from Earth and put them here to continue in all their savage splendour?' asked Varian.

'The Others?'

Bonnard gasped.

'Trizein, you're teasing. The Others destroy life, not save it.' Varian spoke sternly.

Trizein looked unremorseful. 'Everyone is entitled to a bit of a joke. The Theks planted them, of course.'

'Have the Theks planted us, too?' asked Bonnard, scared.

'Good heavens!' Trizein stared at Bonnard, his expression turning from surprise at the idea to delight. 'Do you really think we might be, Varian? When I consider all the investigatory work I must do . . .'

Lunzie and Varian exchanged shocked glances. Trizein would welcome such a development.

'To prove my conclusions of warm-bloodedness. I wonder, Varian, you didn't show me any true saurians, that is to say, any cold-blooded species because if they did develop here as well, as a specialization, of course, it would substantially improve my hypothesis. This world appears to remain consistently hotter than old Earth . . . Well, Varian, what's the matter?'

'We're not planted, Trizein.'

Daunted and disappointed, he looked next to Lunzie who also shook her head.

'Oh, what a pity.' He was so dejected that Varian, despite the seriousness of the moment, had difficulty suppressing her amusement. 'Well, I serve you all fair warning that I do not intend to keep my nose to the data disc and terminal keyboard any more. I shall take time off to investigate my theory. Why didn't anyone think to show me a frame of the animals whose flesh I've been analysing so often? The time I've wasted . . .'

'Analysing animal tissues?' Lunzie spoke first, her eyes catching Varian's in alarm.

'Quite. None of them were toxic, a conclusion now confirmed by our mutual planet of origin. I told Paskutti that so you don't need to be so particular about personal force-screens when in close contact. Where are you keeping the other specimens? Nearby?'

'No. Why do you ask?'

Trizein frowned, having started and diverted himself from any number of lines of thought, and was now being brought up sharp.

'Why? Because I got the distinct impression from Paskutti that he was worried about actual contact with these creatures. Of course, not much can penetrate a heavy-worlder's hide but I could appreciate his worrying that you might get a toxic reaction, Varian. So I assumed that the beasts were nearby, or wounded like that herbivore when we first landed. Did you ever show me a frame of that one?'

'Yes,' Varian replied, absently because her mind was revolving about more pressing identities, like the name of the game the heavy-worlders were playing. 'One of the Hadrasaurs. I think that's what you called it.'

'There were, in fact, quite a variety of Hadrasaur, the crested, the helmeted, the . . .'

'Mabel had a crest,' said Bonnard.

154

'You know, Varian, I think that Kai would be interested in Trizein's identification of Dandy,' said Lunzie.

'You're quite right, Lunzie,' said Varian, moving woodenly towards the lab's communit.

She was relieved when Kai answered instead of Bakkun, though she'd prepared herself to deal with the heavy-worlder, too. She was conscious of Bonnard holding his breath as he wondered what she was going to say, and of Lunzie's calm encouraging expression.

'Trizein has just identified our wild life, Kai, and explained the anomaly. I think you'd better come back to base right now.'

'Varian . . .' Kai sounded irritated.

'Cores are not the only things planted on this stinking ball of mud, Kai, or likely to be planted!'

There was silence on the other end of the communit. Then Kai spoke. 'Very well then, if Trizein thinks it's that urgent. Bakkun can carry on here. The strike is twice the size of the first.'

Varian congratulated him but wondered if he oughtn't to insist that Bakkun return with him. She'd a few questions she'd like to put to that heavy-worlder on the subject of special places and the uses thereof.

CHAPTER TEN

Bakkun made no comment on Kai's recall. He was apparently too engrossed in the intricacies of setting the last core for the shot that would determine the actual size of the pitchblende deposit.

'You'll come back to the base when you finish?' Kai asked as he placed the life-belt for the heavy-worlder by the seismimic.

'If I don't, don't worry. I'll lift over to the secondary camp.'

There was just the slightest trace of emphasis on the personal pronoun. Bakkun's behaviour had been grating on Kai all day. Nothing he could really point to and say Bakkun was being contemptuous or insolent, but the entire work week Kai had sensed a subtle change in the heavy-worlder geologist.

Varian's ambiguous remark about things planted or likely to be planted dominated his nebulous irritation with Bakkun. The co-leader was unlikely to panic over trivia and the fact that she had bothered him on a field trip indicated the seriousness of the matter. What on earth could she mean by that cryptic remark? And how could Trizein's identification of the life forms clear up anomalies?

Maybe there'd been a message from the Theks and Varian had not wanted anyone, patching in on his sled's code, to know. He recalled her exact phrasing. She'd separated Trizein's achievement from the request for him to return. So, it wasn't Trizein's discovery in itself.

Rather than worry needlessly, Kai occupied his mind with estimating the probable wealth of energy materials on this planet, as computed by sites already assessed and the probability of future finds based on the extended orogenic activity in the areas as yet unsurveyed.

By the time he reached the base, he decided that Ireta was undoubtedly one of the richest planets he had ever heard about. It quite cheered him to realize that sooner or later EV would find this out too. Varian, himself and the team members would be rich even by the inflated standards of the Federation Systems. The supportive personnel, and that would have to include the three children if Kai had anything to say about it, should also get bonuses. All three of them had been useful to the expedition. There was Bonnard, now, lugging the power pack from one of the parked sleds. In such small ways, the youngsters had helped contribute to the success of the landing party.

Lunzie was operating the veil and greeted Kai with the information that Varian was in the shuttle. Bonnard, excusing himeslf as he ducked past Kai to deposit the power pack, went out again, heading towards Kai's sled.

'What is Bonnard doing?'

'Checking all the power packs. Inconsistencies have developed.'

'In the power packs? We have been running through them at a terrific rate. Is that why?'

'Probably. Varian's waiting.'

It did not occur to Kai until he was stepping into the shuttle that it was very odd for Lunzie to concern herself with mechanical trivialities. Trizein was at the main view screen, so rapt in his contemplation of frames on browsing herbivores that he was unaware of Kai's entrance.

'Kai?' Varian poked her head around the open access to the pilot's compartment. She beckoned him urgently.

Kai indicated Trizein, silently gesturing whether he should rouse the man. Varian shook her head and motioned him urgently to come.

'What's this all about, Varian?' he said when he had waved the lock closed behind him.

'The heavy-worlders *have* reverted. They took their rest day in fun and games with herbivores and a fang-face. The herbivores they evidently sported with before they killed . . . and ate them.'

Kai's stomach churned in revulsion to her quick words.

'Gaber's rumour was well spread before he spoke to you,

157

Kai. And the heavy-worlders believe him. Or they want to. Those supplies we've been missing, the hours of use I couldn't account for on the big sled, the odd power pack, medical supplies. We're lucky if it isn't mutiny.'

'Go back to the beginning, Varian.' said Kai, sitting heavily in the pilot's chair. He didn't contradict her premise but he did want to see exactly what facts contributed to her startling conclusions.

Varian told him of the morning's hideous discovery, of her conversation with Lunzie and then Trizein's revelation about the planted Earth dinosaurs. She wound up by saying that the heavy-worlders, while not outright uncooperative or insubordinate, had subtly altered in their attitude towards her. Had he noticed anything?

Kai nodded as she finished her summation and, leaning across the board, flipped open the communications unit.

'Is that why Bonnard was removing power packs?'

'Yes.'

'Then you think that a confrontation is imminent?'

'I think if we don't hear from EV tomorrow when you contact the Thek, something will happen. I think our grace period ended last rest day.'

Kai regarded her for a long moment. 'You've worked with them longer than I have. What do you think the heavy-worlders would do?'

'Take over.' She spoke quietly but with calm resignation. 'They are basically better equipped to survive here. We couldn't live off the ... the land's bounty.'

'That's the extreme view. But, if they have believed Gaber and think we've been planted, couldn't their reversion be a way of preparing themselves to be planted?'

'I'd credit that, Kai, if I hadn't seen what games they played last rest day. That frightens the life out of me, frankly. They deliberately ... no, hear me out. It's revolting, I know, but it gives you a better idea of what we'd be up against if we can't stop them. They killed ... *killed* with crude weapons ... five herbivores. Bonnard and I saw another wounded beast, a fang-face, Tyrannosaurus rex, with a tree-size spear stuck in his ribs. Now that creature once ruled old Earth. Nothing could stop him. A heavy-worlder did. For fun!' She took a deep breath. 'Furthermore, by establishing these secondary camps we have given them additional bases. Where are the heavy-worlders right now?'

'Bakkun's on his way back here, presumably. He'd a lift belt. Paskutti and Tardma . . .'

They both heard Lunzie shouting Kai's name. It took them a bare second to realize that Lunzie never shouted unless it was an emergency. They heard the thud and stamp of heavy boots echoing in the outside compartment.

Varian pressed the lock mechanism on the iris just as they heard a heavy hand slap against the outside panel. Kai tapped out a quick sentence on the communit, slapped it into send and cut the power. As he was doing this, Varian pulled the thin, almost undetectable switch that deactivated the main power supply of the ship. An imperceptible blink told them that the ship had switched to auxiliary power, a pack that had strength enough to continue the lighting and minor power drains for several hours.

'If you do not open that lock instantly, we will blast,' said the hard unemotional voice of Paskutti.

'Don't!' Varian managed to get sufficient fear and anxiety in her voice even as she winked, grimaced and shrugged her impotence to Kai.

He nodded acceptance of her decision. It did no one any good for both leaders to be fried alive in the small pilot compartment. He never questioned Paskutti's intention was real. He only hoped that none of the heavy-worlders had noticed the infinitesimal drop in power as Varian had switched from one supply to the other. He and Varian were the only ones to know the fail-safe device that had rendered the shuttle inoperative. Paskutti did not enter the small cabin as the iris opened. After a moment's contemptuous scrutiny of the two leaders, he reached in, grabbed Varian by the front of her ship suit and lifted her out bodily. He let her go, with a negligent force that sent her staggering to crash against the bulkhead. He gave a bark of laughter at the cry she quickly suppressed. As she slowly stood upright, her eyes were flashing with suppressed anger. Her left arm hung at her side.

Kai started to emerge to avoid a similar humiliating display of the heavy-worlders' contempt for other breeds. But Tardma had been waiting her turn. She grabbed his left wrist and twisted it behind his back with such force that he felt the wrist bones splinter. How he managed to keep on his feet and conscious, he didn't know. His abrupt collision with the wall stunned him slightly. A hand supported him under the right arm. Beyond him a girl was sobbing in hopelessness.

Determinedly, Kai shook his head, clearing his mind and initiated the mental discipine that would block the pain. He breathed deeply, from his guts, forcing down the hatred, the impotence, all irrational and emotionally clouding reactions.

The hand that had held him up released him. He was aware that it had been Lunzie, beside him. Her face was white and set, staring straight beyond. From the rate of her respiration, he knew she was practising the same psychic controls. Beyond her, it was Terilla who was weeping in fear and shock.

Kai rapidly glanced about the compartment. Varian was on her feet, struggling to contain a defiance and fury that could only exacerbate their situation. Trizein was next to her, blinking and looking about in confusion as he struggled to absorb this occurrence. Cleiti and Gaber were unceremoniously herded into the shuttle, the cartographer babbling incoherently about this not being the way he had expected matters to proceed, and how dared they treat him with such disrespect.

'Tanegli? Do you have them?' asked Paskutti into his wrist communit. The answer was evidently affirmative for the man nodded at Tardma.

Tanegli? Whom would the heavy-world botanist have – Portegin, Aulia, Dimenon and Margit? As his broken wrist became a numb appendage, Kai's mind became sharper, his perceptions clearer. He felt the beginning of that curious floating sensation that meant mind dominated body. The effect could last up to several hours, depending on how much he drew against the reservoir of strength. He hoped he had enough time. If all the heavy-worlders were assembling here, then Berru would arrive with Triv. When had Bakkun gone then? Or had he assisted Tanegli?

'None of the sleds have power packs,' said Divisti, standing in the lock. 'And that boy is missing.'

Kai and Varian exchanged fleeting glances.

'How did he elude you?' Paskutti was surprised.

Divisti shrugged. 'Confusion. Thought he'd cling to the others.'

So they considered the boy, Bonnard, no threat. Kai looked at Cleiti, hoping she didn't know where Bonnard had gone, hoping the knowledge wasn't clear in her naive face. But her mouth was closed in a firm, defiant line. Her eyes, too, showed suppressed anger; hatred every time she looked towards the heavy-worlders, and disgust for Gaber blubbering beside her.

Terilla had stopped crying but Kai could see the tremors shaking her frail body. A child who preferred plants would find this violence difficult to endure and until Lunzie had achieved her control, she couldn't spare the girl any assistance.

'Start dismantling the lab, Divisti, Tardma.'

The two women nodded and moved to the lab. As they crossed the threshold, Trizean came out of his confusion.

'Wait a minute. You can't go in there. I've experiments and analyses in progress. Divisti, don't touch that fractional equipment. Have you taken leave of your senses?'

'You'll take leave of yours,' said Tardma, pausing at the doorway as the chemist strode towards her. With a cool smile of pleasure, she struck him in the face with a blow that lifted the man off his feet and sent him rolling down the hard deck to lie motionless at Lunzie's feet.

'Too hard, Tardma,' said Paskutti. 'I'd thought to take him. He'd be more useful than any of the other light weights.'

Tardma shrugged. 'Why bother with him anyway? Tanegli knows as much as he does.' She went into the lab with an insolent swing of her hips and shortly emerged with Divisti, each carrying as much equipment as they could with a total disregard for its fragility. Heavy-worlder contempt for light

161

weights evidently extended to their instrumentation. An acrid odour of spilled preservatives and solvents overlaid the air.

With ears now ultra-sensitive, Kai heard the landing whine of a sled. From the west. Tanegli had returned. He heard voices. Bakkun was with Tanegli. Shortly the other light weight geologists were led into the shuttle, Portegin, his head bloody, half-carrying a groggy Dimenon. Aulia and Margit were shoved forward by Bakkun. Triv all but measured his length on the deck, forcefully propelled by Berru who entered behind him, a half-smile of contempt on her face.

Triv reeled to Kai's side, shielding himself from the heavy-worlders by his leader's body. Berru ought not to have been so derisive for Triv now began the breathing exercises that led to the useful Discipline that Kai, Lunzie and Varian were practising. That made four. Kai didn't think either Aulia or Margit had qualified in their training. He knew Portegin and Dimenon were not Disciples. Four wasn't enough to over-power the six heavy-worlders. With luck, though, they might still swing the grim balance back towards hope for the light weights. Kai had no illusions about their situation: the heavy-worlders had mutinied and intended to strip the camp of anything useful, leaving the ship-bred and light weights to fend for themselves, unequipped and unprotected on a hostile, dangerous world.

'All right, Bakkun,' said Paskutti, 'you and Berru go after our allies. We want to make this look right. That communit was still warm when I got here. They must have got a message through to the Theks.' He turned bland eyes on Kai, raising his eyebrows slightly to see if his guess was accurate.

Kai returned the gaze calmly. The heavy-worlder had surprised no telltale expression from him. Paskutti shrugged.

'Tanegli, get the rest of the stores!'

Tanegli was back a second later. 'There aren't any power packs left, Paskutti. I thought you said there were.'

'So there aren't. We've enough in the sleds and the lift-belts for some time. Start loading.'

Tanegli went back into the storehold and, after a noisy few

moments, emerged, staggering under a plasack full of jumbled supplies.

'That clears the storehold, Paskutti.' Tanegli glanced around the staring faces of the captives and, laughing uproariously at some private joke, left.

'No protests, Leader Kai? Leader Varian?' Paskutti's tone and smile were taunting.

'Protests wouldn't do any good, would they?' said Varian. She spoke so calmly that Paskutti frowned as he regarded her. The limp arm had obviously been broken by his mishandling of her, but there was no sign of pain or anger in her voice, merely an amused detachment.

'No, protests wouldn't, Leader Varian. We've had enough of you light weights ordering us about, tolerating us because we're useful.' He used a sneering tone. 'Where would we have fit in your plantation? As beasts of burden? Muscles to be ordered here there and everywhere, and subdued by pap?' He made a cutting gesture with one huge hand.

And then, before any one realized what he intended, he swooped on Terilla, grabbed a handful of the child's hair and yanked her off her feet, letting her dangle at the end of his hand. At Terilla's single, terrified scream, Cleiti jumped up, beating her fists against Paskutti's thick muscular thigh, kicking at his shins. Amused and surprised by such defiance, Paskutti glanced down at Cleiti. Then he raised his fist and landed a casual blow on the top of Cleiti's head. She sank, unconscious, to the deck.

Gaber erupted and dashed at Paskutti who held the cartographer off with his other hand, all the while dangling Terilla by her hair, the girl's eyes stretched to slits by the tautness of his grasp.

'Tell me, Leader Varian, Leader Kai, did you send a message to the Theks? One second's delay and I'll break her back across my knee.'

'We sent a message,' replied Kai promptly. 'Mutiny. Heavyworlders.'

'Did you ask for help from our estimable supervisors?' asked

Paskutti, giving Terilla a shake when he thought Kai deliberated too long in answering.

'Help? From Theks?' asked Varian, her eyes never leaving the helplessly swinging girl. 'It would take them several days to ponder the message. By then, your . . . operation will be all over, won't it? No, we merely reported a condition.'

'Only to the Theks?'

Now Kai saw what Paskutti needed to know: whether or not a message had also been beamed up to the satellite. If so, he would have to alter his 'operation' in accordance.

'Only to the Theks,' said Kai, the mind-dominated part of his emotions wanting to add 'now release the girl'.

'You know what you need to know,' screamed Gaber, still attempting to reach Paskutti and make him release Terilla. 'You'll kill the child. Release her! Release her! You told me there'd be no violence. No one hurt! You've killed Trizein, and if you don't let go of that child . . .'

Paskutti casually swatted Gaber into silence, the cartographer hit the deck with a terrible thud and rolled to one side. Terilla was dropped in a heap by Cleiti. Kai couldn't tell if the girl had been killed by the mishandling. He glanced surreptitiously at Lunzie who was staring at the girls. Some relaxation about the woman's eyes reassured him: the girls were alive.

Beside him, Triv had completed the preliminaries to Discipline. Now he, too, would wait until his strength could be of use. The hardest part was the waiting until such time as this controlled inner strength would be channelled into escape. Kai breathed low in the diaphragm, willing himself to the patience required to endure this hideous display of brute strength and cruelty.

Dimenon was rousing but, although he moaned in pain, Lunzie did not attend him. Margit, Aulia and Portegin kept their eyes front, trying not to focus on scenes they could neither stop nor change.

Tanegli came storming up the ramp to the shuttle, his face contorted with anger, a man controlled by his emotions, no longer the calm rational botanist, interested in growing things.

'There isn't a power pack in any of the sleds,' he told Paskutti but he strode right up to Varian, grabbing her by both arms and shaking her. Kai willed her to feign unconsciousness. Such handling might impair any chance of that broken shoulder healing properly.

'Where did you hide them, you tight-assed bitch?' he cried.

'Watch your strength, Tanegli. Don't break her neck yet,' said Paskutti, stepping forward in his urgency to arrest the angry man.

Tanegli visibly pulled back some force of the blow he had levelled at Varian. Nevertheless, her head rolled sharply backwards but as she righted herself, her eyes were still open. The marks of Tanegli's fingers were vivid weals on her cheek.

'Where did you hide the power packs?'

'She's broken her left shoulder. Use that as goad,' said Paskutti. 'Not too much . . . just enough. Can't have her passing out with pain. These light weights can't take much.'

'Where? Varian, where?' Tanegli accompanied each word with a twist to her left arm.

Varian cried out. To Kai's ears, the echo was false since, in the throes of Discipline, Varian wouldn't feel pain right now.

'I didn't hide them. Bonnard did.'

Margit and Aulia gasped at this craven betrayal of the boy.

'Go get him, Tanegli. Find out where those power packs are or we'll be backing the supplies out of here. Bakkun and Berru will have started the drive. Nothing can stop it once it starts.' Paskutti twitched with a sense of urgency now.

'She'd know where he is. Tell me, where? Varian?'

Varian suddenly hung limp in Tanegli's grip. He let her drop to the deck with a disgusted oath and strode to the open lock. Kai heard three more steps before the man stopped, shouting for Bonnard to come. Then Tanegli called for Divisti and Tardma to help him search for the boy.

Paskutti looked down at Varian's crumpled figure. Kai hoped that the man didn't suspect that she was only pretending. An expression close to the snarl of a fang-face crossed the heavy-worlder's face, but he was expressionless again when he turned to Kai.

'March!' Paskutti gestured peremptorily to the lock. He motioned to Lunzie and the others to move; with flicks of his forefinger he indicated that each was to carry one of the unconscious ones. 'Into the main dome, all of you!' he ordered.

As they crossed the compound, Dandy was lying dead in his pen, back broken. Kai was glad neither Cleiti nor Terilla would see their pet. The ground was littered with scattered tapes, charts, exposed records and splintered discs. Inadvertently he trod on one of Terilla's careful drawings of a plant. Forcing deep breaths from his diaphragm, he controlled the fury he felt at such wanton destruction.

The main dome had been stripped of everything useful. The unconscious were laid on the floor, the others motioned to stand by the farthest arc from the iris lock.

Outside, the search for Bonnard continued. Paskutti was now glancing first at his wrist chrono and then at the plains beyond the force-screen.

Kai's heightened hearing caught the faint sound of his name. Carefully he turned his head and saw Lunzie staring at him, saw her imperceptibly indicate that he was to look outside. By shifting slightly he could see out, could see two dots in the sky, the black line beneath, a tossing black line, a moving black line and then he knew what the heavy-worlders had planned to do.

The force-screen was strong enough to keep out ordinary dangers but not the massed attack of stampeded creatures. The camp's advantage of height above the plain and forest would be cancelled. The heavy-worlders were herding the animals right up where they wanted them to do their damage.

The Theks, receiving Kai's message, might react to it . . . in a few days' time. They might, if the thinking spirit moved them, send one of the younger Theks to investigate. But Kai doubted it. The Theks would rightly consider that any intervention of theirs would arrive too late to affect the outcome of the mutiny.

The light weights would have to effect their own salvation. The heavy-worlders would have to leave the compound soon,

Would it be soon enough? And how would they leave their scorned captives? Could Bonnard stay out of their grasp?

Paskutti's fingers twitched. He glanced, almost apprehensively at the wrist chrono, squinted at the oncoming black line.

'Tanegli? Haven't you found that boy?' Paskutti's bellow deafened ears made sensitive by the Discipline.

'He's hidden. We can't find him, or the power packs!' Tanegli was raging with frustration.

'Come back, then. We're wasting time.' Paskutti was not at all pleased with this unexpected check to his plans. The look he turned on the limp figure of Varian was ominous. 'How did she know?' he asked Kai. 'Bakkun thought something was up when she used such a trivial excuse to bring you back early.'

'She found the place where you spent rest day. And the wounded fang-face you couldn't kill.' Kai's instinct was to continue to protect Bonnard as long as he could from possible retaliation. If they all died, the boy couldn't last on his own on Ireta. He'd have to seek what refuge the heavy-worlders would offer him.

'Bonnard! I told Bakkun he took a risk letting the boy see the arena.' Paskutti's face reflected many emotions now, contempt, supercilious disdain, satisfaction in past performances. His upper lip drew back from his teeth in a travesty of a smile. 'You wouldn't have appreciated our rest day. No matter,' Paskutti glanced down the valley. 'The rehearsal has paid dividends . . . for us!'

The sun in its brief evening appearance, lighting the plain so that Kai discerned the bobbing bodies of the herbivores inexorably moving toward the encampment. The other heavy-worlders now congregated about the lock, their faces for once flushed with exertion and shiny with sweat.

'He's gone to earth,' said Tanegli in a savage tone, glaring at Kai. 'And all the power packs.'

'We've no more time to look. Move the sleds out of the direct line of the stampede. Be quick about it. Do you all have lift-belts? Good. Then keep up and out of trouble until the stampede has passed.'

'What about the shuttle?'

'It should be all right,' said Paskutti, glancing at the vessel perched above the encampment on its ledge. 'Move!'

The others did, in great leaping strides towards the sled park.

Paskutti stood in the iris opening, hands on his belt, glancing with unconcealed pleasure at the docile captives. Kai knew that the moment of ultimate danger was *now*! Would Paskutti seal them into the dome, conscious and cruelly aware of their fate? Or would he stun them?

His essentially cruel nature won.

'I leave you now, to your fitting end. Trampled by creatures, stupid, foolish vegetarians like yourselves. The only one of you strong enough to stand up to us a mere boy.'

He closed the iris lock and the thud of his fist against the plaswall told Kai that he had shattered the controls.

Varian, suddenly mobile, was peering over the bottom of the far window, her left arm dangling uselessly.

'Varian?' said Lunzie, doing something to the still body of Trizein. The man groaned suddenly, shocked back to consciousness. Lunzie moved to Terilla and Cleiti, nodding to herself as she administered restorative sprays.

'He's at the veil,' reported Varian in a low voice. 'He's opened it. He's left it open. I can see two others sky-borne. Bakkun and Berru probably. We ought to have a few moments when the herd tops the last rise when they won't be able to see anything.'

'Triv!' Kai gestured and the geologist followed him to the rear arc of the dome, motioning the others to one side.

Kai's sensitized fingers felt the fine seam of the plastic skin. Triv placed his fingertips further up the seam. They both took the requisite deep breaths, called out and ripped the tough fabric apart.

Lunzie had the two girls on their feet, staggering but conscious enough to stand. She turned to help Trizein.

'Where could Bonnard have gone to, Kai?' asked Varian in a tight voice that betrayed an anxiety not even the Discipline could mask.

168

'Well hidden enough to elude the heavy-worlders. Safe enough from what's coming. Now,' and he turned to his comrades. 'We cannot panic, but we must wait until the exact moment when the sky-borne heavy-worlders cannot see us or they will merely stun us down. Margit, Aulia, Portegin, you're all able to run?' They nodded. 'Lunzie, you'll take Terilla? Is Gaber dead? Well, Aulia, you and Portegin help Cleiti. Triv will carry Trizein. I'll help Dimenon. Varian, can you manage?'

'As well as you. I'll back us up.'

'I will,' said Kai, shaking his head and looking at her hanging arm.

'No, you've Dimenon. I'll manage.' She glanced out the window again.

It did not take sensitive hearing now to hear the approaching stampede. It did take stern control to remain calm.

'There are four in the sky now,' said Varian, 'and the beasts have reached the narrow part of the approach. Get ready.'

Aulia stifled a cry of fear.

'Everyone, breath deeply from the diaphragm,' said Lunzie, 'and when we give you the word, to go, yell and *run*! Keep yelling. It stirs the adrenalin.'

'I don't need any more,' said Margit in a tremulous but defiant voice.

The thunder was deafening, the very plastic shook under their feet. Aulia was trembling so noticeably, Kai wondered if she could stand the strain.

'NOW!'

Their concerted yells would never reach the sky-borne heavy-worlders. Margit was right, there was no need of additional adrenalin. The sight of the bobbing heads of the crested dinosaurs, bearing down on them, was sufficient to have lent wings to anyone. Dimenon, yelling at the top of his lungs, wrestled from Kai's support and outdistanced others as he made for the shuttle. Kai slowed his pace until Varian was abreast of him. Then the two leaders matched strides in the wake of the others, across a compound shuddering with the vibrations of the stampede. They vaulted the first terrace of the incline, nearly running down Lunzie as she angled Trizein into the lock. Varian steadied the physician as Kai fumbled for the lock control. The first of the herbivores reached the force-screen.

A high-pitched scream pierced through the overlying thunder and bellowing as the screen burned, flashed blue fire and broke, with a terrible whining. The bodies of herbivores flowed into the compound, and then the mass behind the forerunners surged up, over the fallen and onward. The iris closed on that scene. Only the noise and vibration did not seem to diminish inside the shuttle, telling of the chaos, death and destruction outside.

As one now, Kai and Varian moved through the panting, shocked members of the expedition to the pilot cabin. Varian fumbled for the hidden switch to restore power to the shuttle. Kai started to sit at the console and stopped.

'Paskutti took no chances on another message,' he told Varian, looking at the wreckage of the board.

'What about manoeuvring?'

'That's still intact. He knew what circuits to break all right.'

They felt the shuttle move, heard something banging dully against the outer hull.

'They outdid themselves with the stampede,' said Varian with an amused chuckle. She heard the startled exclamations from the main compartment and put her head around the frame.

'It'll take more than herbivores to dent the shuttle ceramic. Don't worry. But I would sit down.' She slid into the other seat, moving her useless arm out of her way when it flopped against the backrest. 'As soon as the stampede has stopped, we'd better make our move.'

'Bonnard?' asked Kai.

'Bonnard!' Portegin echoed the name in a glad cry in the main cabin. 'Bonnard! Kai, Varian. He got in!'

The leaders saw the boy emerging from the lab, his ship suit dusty and stained, his face drawn with a sudden maturity.

'I thought this was the safest place after I saw Paskutti

moving you out. But I wasn't sure who had come back in. Am I glad it's you!'

Cleiti was embracing her friend, weeping with relief. Terilla, bedded down by Trizein, called his name over and over, not quite believing his appearance. Bonnard gently put Cleiti's clinging hands to one side and walked to the leaders.

'They'll never find those power packs, Varian. Never! But I thought you'd be killed when I saw Paskutti lock the dome. He smashed the control so I didn't see how I could get you out in time. So . . . I . . . hid!' The boy burst into tears of shame.

'You did exactly as you should, Bonnard. Even to hiding!'

Another shift of the shuttle sent everyone rocking.

'It's going to fall,' cried Aulia, hands over her ears.

'It could, but it won't crack,' said Kai, feeling the same post-crisis elation that had made Varian chuckle. 'Stay calm. We've succeeded so far. We'll survive!'

CHAPTER ELEVEN

Although Kai's wrist chrono showed that only twenty minutes had elapsed from the moment they had reached the pilot's cabin, it had seemed an age of repeated shocks and jolts until all external noise ceased.

After a moment of silence, Kai opened the iris lock enough to peer out. And saw nothing but mottled coarse furred hide. He stepped back, gesturing for Varian to look out.

'Buried alive in Hadrasaurs,' she said, irrepressible. Her eyes were very bright, her face lined with the strain of maintaining Discipline over the agony of her crushed and broken shoulder. 'Open wider. They're too big to fall in.'

With a wider view, they achieved only the vision of more bodies, darkness beyond. Kai reluctantly decided that they'd have to send Bonnard, who was agile and small enough, to assess the new position of the shuttle. Bonnard was warned to keep a low profile in case the heavy-worlders were about.

'You might remember that it is now full dark,' Lunzie said. 'They don't have good night vision. *If* they are out there.'

'Where else would they be?' demanded Aulia, hysteria in her shaking voice. 'Gloating! Delighted with themselves. I've never liked working with heavy-worlders. They always think they're abused and misused and they're really not good for anything but heavy muscle work.'

'Oh, do be quiet, Aulia,' said Lunzie. 'Go on with you, Bonnard, see if we have a clear passage for the shuttle. I'll be as glad to put a lot of distance between myself and the heavy-worlders as anyone else in this shuttle.' She handed him a night-mask and gave him a reassuring and approving grin.

'Portegin, would you check the control panel's circuitry?' asked Kai. 'Varian, let Lunzie see to that arm now we've a spare moment.'

'If, after that, Lunzie gets a crack at your hand, Leader Kai,'

'No "ifs" about it. I do you first, him next,' said Lunzie, reaching for her belt pouch. 'At least they left me something to work with.'

'Why bother patching any of us?' demanded Aulia, sinking to the deck, head in her arms. '*We* can't last long on this planet. Paskutti was right about that. And *they've* got everything we *need*!'

'Not everything. They left us the synthesizer,' said Varian with a snort. 'Couldn't take that, built into the shuttle as it is.'

'There's no power to run it. You heard Tanegli.'

'Bonnard hid the sleds' packs. They'll do for the synthesizer.'

'That's only delaying the inevitable,' cried Aulia. 'We'll all die once the packs are drained. There's no way to recharge them.'

'Kai got a message out to the Theks,' said Varian, hoping to forestall Aulia's imminent hysterics.

'The Theks!' Aulia burst out laughing, a shrill, mirthless sound. Portegin came striding out of the pilot's cabin and slapped her smartly across the face.

'That's enough of that, you silly girl. You always do give up too easily.'

'She has brought up a few harsh truths,' said Margit in a weary voice. 'Once the synthesizer is useless, we're as good as . . .'

'We can always sleep it,' said Kai.

'I didn't realize that this expedition had cryogenics,' said Margit but hope brightened her expression.

'This may be a small expedition, but it has all the basics. Or had,' replied Kai who, finding the proper space between the bulkheads, pressed the release and showed them the hidden recess with the cryogenic supplies.

'But if Portegin could fix the communit, we wouldn't have to cold sleep,' said Aulia, her face also showing relief, 'we could just beam EV—'

'No, and I might as well tell you right now,' said Portegin, his expression grim, 'I can't fix that panel. Not without the spare parts which *they've* removed.'

173

'I knew it,' said Aulia, beginning to weep in the silence that followed Portegin's announcement.

'You know nothing,' said Portegin sharply, 'so shut up.'

'Sleep is what we all need, right now. Regular sleep,' said Lunzie, sparing Kai a significant glance.

Once Discipline had worn off, the four of them would need a full day's rest before they could recover from the necessary abuse of their systems. With Aulia in such a state, and the others certain to react in one way or another to the shock of their experiences, their escape from the heavy-worlders would be meaningless if Kai and Varian could not maintain control.

'Sleep?' demanded Margit. 'Under what's up there?' She pointed to the ceiling of the shuttle and shuddered.

'Look at it this way, Margit,' said Dimenon, 'we're beautifully secure. Even heavy-worlders will have to sweat to clean that . . . how should I phrase it – carrion? debris – away.'

'No, Dimenon. We're not staying here,' said Kai. 'Our best escape is best made now, under cover of the dark, so that when the heavy-worlders return, as I'm sure they will, they will presume that the entire shuttle is still here, buried under the stampede.'

'The carrion eaters of Ireta work swiftly,' Varian said, perspiration beading her face as Lunzie continued her repairs on the broken shoulder. 'But they've enough out there for days . . .'

Someone retched.

'Which gives us a certain leeway before they discover the shuttle is gone. *If* we move tonight.'

'Where do you suggest we move to?' asked Portegin in a dry tone.

'That's no problem,' said Dimenon with a snort. 'We've a whole bloody planet.'

'Not really,' said Kai. 'And they want this shuttle. They need it – if only for the synthesizer and the main power unit. Once they've found it's gone, they're going to look for it. And look hard. They've tracers on the sleds, and while they don't have the power packs,' here he favoured Bonnard with an admiring grin, 'they're strong enough to dismantle the units and use 'em while they belt-lift. And find us.'

'Not if we're well hidden,' said Varian, emphasizing the 'well' in a voice that held a ripple of amusement. 'No heavyworlder would think of it. And there'd be a lot of other lifeform readings to confuse them.'

Kai regarded Varian, his mind rushing through the possible locations, unable to guess what she had thought of although Varian looked at him as if he ought to know.

'Our rest day was a rehearsal, too, though we couldn't know it at the time.'

'The giffs?'

'Yes, that cave where I found the dead egg. It was enormous inside, and dry. Why it was abandoned, I can't figure. But it should do us.'

Kai wanted to grab her in his arms, kiss and hug her for that suggestion but it was neither the time nor place.

'That's exactly the right place, Varian. We'd even register the same as the adult giffs. And the kids as juveniles! Varian, that's . . , that's . . .'

'The best idea we've heard all day,' said Lunzie, finishing when words failed Kai. There was as much relief in her voice as in Kai's. Varian beamed at the reception of her solution.

'Fine. We'll hole up there . . .' and he ducked as Lunzie swung at him for his pun, 'get a good night's sleep and then do some heavy evaluation. I did, and don't forget this, my friends, get that message off to the Theks . . .' He held up his hand as Aulia opened her mouth to renew her arguments to aid from that source, 'and as one of them is an old friend of my family's on the ARCT-10, I think I can promise that the message will not be ignored.'

Aulia may not have been convinced but Kai saw that others were willing to rest some confidence in that fact.

'Where has Bonnard got to?' asked Varian, shuddering as Lunzie finished her manipulation on her shoulder. 'He ought to have been long back.'

'I'll go,' said Triv and was out of the lock before either leader could protest.

'Now, Leader Kai,' said Lunzie, indicating it was his turn at her hands.

'Margit, would you break out some peppers for us all?' said Kai, surrendering his broken wrist to Lunzie and diverting his thoughts. 'I don't think they got what was in the locker in the pilot's compartment.'

'A pepper?' Margit moved with alacrity to the forward compartment, Aulia right behind her. 'That's the second best idea I've heard today. Pray Krim they didn't get the peppers! Ah, the locker's untouched! Leave off, Aulia, pass them out to the others, first!' Her voice had turned hard.

'You know, this is the first time I've ever seen Leaders required to use Discipline,' said Dimenon, cracking the seal on the can Aulia had handed him. She was drinking hers as she passed others the restoratives. 'I'm aware that a Leader has to have the Training to lead, but I'd never seen it working. I couldn't figure out what had got into you, Varian, when you let them beat admissions out of you.'

'I had to play the coward,' said Varian, taking a long swig at her pepper. 'Dead Disciples are no use to anyone. I'd guessed that Bonnard would be smart enough to hide. I do wish he'd get back now, though.'

They all heard the noises at the lock. Kai slipped his half-sealed wrist from Lunzie's grasp and moved quickly to the lock, good hand poised in a clenched fist. Portegin and Dimenon joined him, their bare hands cocked back.

'I found him,' Triv said, poking his head through the half-opened iris. 'He'd been stacking all the power packs at the edge of . . . the dead beasts. He's gone for the others now.' He handed three power packs through the lock to Portegin. 'He says the heavy-worlders have started a fire on the ridge beyond us. We'll be able to slide the shuttle to our left, up the hill and they shouldn't see us. Dead and dying herbivores are hill high in the compound. It's going to take some time before *they* realize neither we nor the shuttle are buried here.'

'Good,' said Kai and motioned Triv to return to help Bonnard. 'We can be gone without a trace left for them to follow or find, bless this ceramic hull.'

Once the resourceful boy and Triv had swung the power packs safely into the shuttle, they closed the lock. Kai and Varian took Bonnard into the pilot's compartment where he could diagram the shuttle's position and the clearest way up the hill.

Paskutti's fist had wrecked the outside view screens as well as the communication unit so manoeuvres would be blind. Not, Varian pointed out, that they could have seen all that much even with night-masks and they couldn't, under the circumstances, use the shuttle's exterior spotbeams. Both Kai and Varian could recall the co-ordinates for the inland sea without the tapes now spread across the compound's littered floor.

Triv and Dimenon synthesized enough padding to cushion the wounded on the bare plastic deck, and had set Margit and Aulia to clear up the worst of the spillage in Trizein's laboratory. He was unconscious again, the strain having been excessive for a man of his years. Lunzie thought he might have suffered a heart seizure as a result of the brutal treatment.

Manoeuvring on the bare minimum of power, Kai and Varian, each with one good hand, eased the shuttle out from under its burden of Hadrasaur corpses, up the hill and onto a course for the inland sea.

During the trip, Lunzie synthesized a hyper-saturated tonic to reduce the effects of delayed shock and made certain every single person took their dose, either as a drink or a spray. With Triv and Dimenon's assistance, Portegin began to raid all unnecessary circuits to see if he could jury rig even an outgoing signal.

When they reached the inland sea, Kai hovered the shuttle while Varian, the lock iris partly open, shouted verbal instructions to the terrace they had happily occupied that rest day, it seemed so long ago. When the lock was half a metre above the terrace, Varian and Triv jumped down. They would have to guide the shuttle into the cave, feeding Kai directions over their wrist communits. Since the heavy-worlders were sure of their deaths in the dome, it was unlikely any of them would be listening in on their own units.

The mouth of the cave was not large enough to accept the central bulge of the shuttle, but, by steadily pressing in against the rock, they forced a way through, ignoring the score marks on the ceramic skin of the shuttle.

Varian, standing in the darkness of the terrace, couldn't understand why the grating noise and vibrations hadn't aroused the entire population of the cliff but no crested head emerged to investigate.

Triv lowered Varian down to the cave by belt line. Then, having secured one end on a rocky spur on the terrace, he joined her. The shuttle was far enough inside the cave not to be immediately visible. But Triv and Varian gathered up masses of dried vegetation and threw them in camouflage over the stern of the shuttle. Dimenon, Margit and Portegin came out to help, spattering the top and sides with moistened cave dung.

It didn't take long but everyone was relieved to be inside the shuttle, with the iris closed behind them. Then the others settled themselves with what comfort they could find.

'You are going to rest, aren't you, Lunzie,' asked Kai, hunkering down by her side as she tended Trizein.

She gave a snort. 'I'll have no option as soon as Discipline releases. But Trizein should be all right. It's natural for his system to seek repair in rest. And there won't be anything to disturb him. How're you?' she asked bluntly, glancing at sealed wrist and then more intently at his eyes.

'I'm still under Discipline, but not for much longer.'

She filled her spray gun. 'I'll give everyone else slightly more sedation than necessary. That'll give us a chance for enough rest.'

She moved about the cabin then, administering the spray.

Varian tapped Kai on the shoulder.

'We've accommodation forward, Kai.'

He glanced round the recumbent forms and then followed her, gratefully lowering himself on the deck on the padding. Thin but thermal lined sheets had been fashioned and ought, he thought, to suffice. The ship would keep the interior temperature at a comfortable level for sleepers. Lunzie and Triv joined them and settled down, too.

'It could be worse, Kai,' said the physician, as if she read his thoughts as he stared down the bare cabin at the other sleepers. 'We only lost Gaber and that fool asked for it with his tardy heroics.'

'Terilla and Cleiti?' asked Varian.

'Were mauled about, but no more. Worse for the psyche and the body. One doesn't wish that sort of treatment for anyone . . .' Lunzie grimaced.

'I'm more concerned about their reaction towards Kai and myself when we seemed not to defend or protect them . . .'

Lunzie smiled. 'They understand that! I know Cleiti's parents are Disciples and I suspect Terilla's mother is. What they can't understand is the heavy-worlders' metamorphosis into brutal, cruel temperaments.' Lunzie sighed. 'All in all, I think we comported ourselves rather well, considering the odds against us and the unexpectedness of that mutiny.'

Suddenly her body sagged and she sighed again, with relief.

'I'm off,' she said, fumbling with shaking hands for the sedative gun. 'Are you two ready for it?'

'Leave it,' said Kai. 'We can do ourselves.'

Triv offered his arm to the physician. 'I'm off it, too, Lunzie.' The release of Discipline was obvious in the grey that seeped into his complexion. He was nearly asleep before Lunzie had fully administered the drug. 'I'll wake first,' he mumbled, and his head dropped to one side.

Lunzie snorted as she turned the spray on herself. 'Not if I beat you to it, my friend. That's the marvel of Discipline, or is it the bane, working even when you don't want it to.' She exhaled raggedly and closed her eyes. 'You've done well, leaders! You can rest easy on that score. Never met a . . . bet . . . ter . . .'

Varian chuckled. 'You might know Lunzie would leave a compliment unspoken.' She kept her voice low though not even a repeat stampede would have wakened the physician or the other sleepers. 'Kai? Will Tor respond?'

'He's more likely to than any other Thek.'

'When?'

Discipline must be leaving her, Kai thought, hearing the anxiety in her roughened voice. He took her good hand in his and carried it to his lips. She smiled, despite her worry, at the caress.

'I'd say it will be a week before he could possibly arrive. I think we can hold them together that long, don't you?'

'After today, yes, I think we can. But, Kai, they don't know we've no contact with EV. Thek help is grand but pretty poor consolation because it's debatable.'

'I know. It is, however, contact.' He felt Discipline leaving him, felt the massive fatigue, like an intolerable weight, press down on his abused body. Muhlah, but he'd be almighty stiff when he woke.

'Are you released, Kai? You look it.'

He laughed softly, noting the drain of colour from her face. He lifted the spray gun.

'Wait.' She raised herself on her good elbow and kissed him on the lips, a gentle kiss but nonetheless an accolade. 'I don't want to fall asleep kissing you.'

'I appreciate that consideration,' he said. And gave her a quick, affectionate kiss, pressing the spray against her arm, and then his own. He arranged his limbs and just had time to curl his fingers about hers before sleep overtook him.

CHAPTER TWELVE

Kai was not the only stiff one when they finally woke. And Lunzie had roused before Triv, which put her in a good mood. Trizein was improving, she told the leaders as she handed them each beakers of a steaming nutritious broth. Her own special recipe, she said, guaranteed to circulate blood through abused muscles and restore tissue to normal.

'You'll need to be limber. We've got to have more for the synthesizer to masticate or I won't have enough of my brew to revive the others.'

Kai sipped carefully of the hot liquid. Lunzie had not misrepresented its effectiveness. As the warmth descended to his stomach, he could almost feel the loosening of his stiff muscles. He did have to apply slight Disciplinary controls to reduce the ache in his wrist.

'How long did we sleep?'

'I'd say we made it around the chrono and half again,' Lunzie said, glancing at her wrist bracelet. 'I *know* we didn't sleep a mere twelve hours or I've lost my knack at pulling sedatives into a sprayer. Which I haven't.'

'How long before the others rouse?' asked Triv, who was now awake.

'I'd say we have another clear hour or so before the dead arise.'

'A little recon?' Triv asked the two leaders.

'Just remember,' said Lunzie at her driest, 'you've none of your force-belts anymore. Don't fall.'

From reflex action, Kai found himself reaching for the stun locker door and saw its open, empty shelves.

'Yes, indeed,' said Varian with a wry laugh, 'the cupboard is bare.'

'And all we've got is bare hands . . .'

'One a piece,' said Varian with a second laugh.

'Remember, you won't be able to use full Discipline today,' Lunzie cautioned. 'I trust the need will not arise.'

'I doubt it. The giffs aren't aggressive,' said Varian, settling her hand comfortably against her body before stepping through the iris. 'Another reason why this is a perfect hideaway.'

A scant few minutes later, as they peered past the mouth of their retreat, she revised her statement.

'Well, there are a few drawbacks.' She squinted down at the waves beating against the foot of their twenty metre high cliff. To either side was an expanse of sheer rock. The line Triv had secured from the terrace flapped in the light breeze. Looking up, Varian could see the giffs flying. 'At least there's nothing but giffs airborne,' she added with an exaggerated sigh of relief.

'And nothing for the synthesizer either,' said Kai, trying to recall exactly what lay beyond the terrace and the rock-shelf on which the giffs dropped their catch.

Triv had gone to the rear of the cavern and came back now, a sheaf of dried grasses in each hand. 'There's lots more of this, dried, but they'll provide some substance for the synthesizer.'

'There's forest beyond the cliffs,' said Varian, thoughtfully, frowning as she concentrated. 'Blast but we rely too much on tapes and not enough on our own recall.'

'C'mon, don't fuss yourself, Varian. We'll collect grasses at least. Triv, how are you at climbing up ropes?'

'I'll learn but I suspect it's the sort of thing Bonnard will do extremely well,' he said with a grin, tesing the rope and then peering up its length, his expression dubious.

Lunzie was not pleased with the grasses. Fresh they'd have been perfect but there was no telling how long they'd been lying about the cavern. Couldn't they get some fresh green — even tree tops?

Tree tops were about all they could reach, Triv informed the leaders when he and the youngsters had returned from their foraging. There was a tantalizing view of fruiting trees beyond a narrow but impassable canyon which separated the main cliffs from the forest beyond. At least from the terrace level which was, at the moment, all they could reach.

'The giffs watched us,' Bonnard told Varian and Kai, 'just like they did that rest day. Just watched.'

'And I watched the skies for anything else,' said Terilla, a curiously bitter note to her soft voice and an unsettling hardness to her face.

'Them?' Bonnard dismissed the heavy-worlders with a fine scorn. 'They're still thinking we've all been smashed flat in the dome!'

There was, the two leaders noted with wry approval, a decided smugness about Bonnard to which he was, in fact, entitled. He, alone, had managed to evade and discommode the heavy-worlders, despite their physical superiority.

'Let us devoutly hope that they continue in that delusion for a few more days,' said Kai. 'Until Tor has a chance to arrive. Can you manage another trip today?' he asked, eying the pile of fresh greens and estimating the finished, synthesized result.

Triv's answer was to turn back to the rope and begin the ascent, the others queuing to follow him.

'Morale's very good,' Kai murmured to Varian.

'Now!' Varian's single bitter word reminded Kai that morale was fickle.

To bolster his own spirits he sought Portegin, working in Trizein's looted laboratory on a pile of matrix slabs and the damaged console panel which he had removed from the piloting compartment.

'I don't know if I can fix the communit, even if I pirate every matrix circuit we've got and do field links,' the man said, running his fingers through his short hair. 'They didn't leave us so much as a sealing unit and these connections are too fine to be done by hand.'

'Could you rig a locator signal on the Theks', or even the ARCT-10's frequencies?'

'Sure,' and Portegin brightened to be able to give a positive response.

'Do so, then, preferably one the heavy-worlders can't tap.'

'They've got to have power first, more power than they've got on their wrist units,' said Portegin, grinning with a touch of malice.

Kai moved on, checking futilely in the storage compartments in the hopes that something useful had been dropped by the heavy-worlders. He thanked providence for the ceramic hull of the shuttle which would not show up on the detectors the heavy-worlders possessed. The minor amounts of metal in the ship would easily be misread as ore in the cliffs. He tried again to remember if he and Varian had done much talking about the giffs in the hearing of any of the heavy-worlders. And remembered the tapes! Fighting the frantic pulse of fear, he also remembered the tangled, destroyed tape cannisters strewn about the compound and now buried beneath megatons of dead beasts. Supercilious of the light weights as the mutineers were, doubtless they had chucked tapes registered by either himself or Varian as being intrinsically useless. Kai forced himself to believe that possibility.

Everyone was busy at something, he noted. Triv and the youngsters were on the foraging party, Aulia was sweeping the main cabin with a broom made of short stiff grasses, Dimenon and Margit were hauling water up the cliff in an all too small improvised bucket.

'Try a piece,' said Varian, offering him a brownish slab. 'It's not bad,' she added as he broke off a corner and began to chew it.

'Dead grass?'

'Hmmm.'

'I've eaten worse. Very dry, isn't it.'

'Dry grass, but it's bearable. There'll be plenty of this junk, so Lunzie is good enough to reassure us.' Then her expression altered to one of distaste. 'Trouble is, it uses a lot of power, and water, which uses power, too, to be purified.'

Kai shrugged. Food they had to have, and water.

'We need at least a week for Tor to reply.'

Varian regarded him for a long moment. 'Exactly what good will Tor's appearance do us?'

'The heavy-worlders' mutiny, or I should say their success,

depends on *our* silence. That's why they rigged our "deaths" so carefully, in case we hadn't been planted. Why they'd believe Gaber is beyond me, but . . .' Kai shrugged. Then he grinned. 'Heavy-worlders are big, but no one is bigger than a Thek. And no one in the galaxy deliberately provokes Thek retaliation. Their concept of Discipline is a trifle . . . more permanent . . . than ours. Once we have Thek support, we can resume out interrupted work.'

Varian considered this reassurance and, for some reason that irked Kai, did not appear as consoled as she ought.

'Well, Lunzie estimates we've got four weeks of power at the current rate of use.'

'That's good, but I'm not happy about four weeks stuck in this cavern.'

'I know what you mean.'

Their refuge was twice as long as the shuttle craft's twenty-one metres, and half again as wide, but it ended in a rather daunting rock fall which may have been why the cave was abandoned by the giffs. There was not much space for privacy, and they couldn't risk lighting the innermost section which would have lessened the cramping.

By the time the quick tropic night had darkened their refuge, Portegin had succeeded in rigging a locator which he and Triv mounted in a crevice just outside the cliff mouth. After a final look to be sure that the stern of the shuttle was sufficiently camouflaged, Kai and Varian ordered everyone back into the shuttle. By the simple expedient of having Lunzie introduce a sedative into the evening ration of water, everyone was soon too sleepy to worry about confinement or boredom.

The next day Kai and Varian sent everyone but the convalescent Trizein out to gather greenery. They estimated that they had this second day secure from any search by the heavy-worlders: possibly a third but they could take no chances.

The third day, apart from drawing water at dawn, was spent inside the cave. Portegin and Triv contrived a screen of branches and grass which could be used to secure a sentinel at the cave entrance, to warn of any sign of either search from the heavy-worlders or, hopefully, the arrival of a Thek capsule. The angle of vision from the screen was limited but would have to suffice.

The fourth day passed uneventfully but by the fifth, everyone was beginning to show the effects of close quartering. The sixth day Lunzie doctored the morning beverage so that everyone except herself, Triv and the two leaders were kept dozy. That meant that they had to maintain the watch themselves and draw the water at dawn and again at dusk.

By the end of the seventh day, Kai had to admit that Tor had not rushed to their assistance.

'What is our alternative?' Triv asked calmly at the informal conference the four Disciples held.

'There's cold sleep,' said Lunzie, looking rather relieved when Kai and Varian nodded.

'That's the sensible last resort,' said Triv, fiddling with a square of grasses he'd been idly weaving. 'The others're going to become more and more dissatisfied with seclusion in this cave. Of course, once there aren't any messages for EV, they'll be bound to investigate.' Something in their manner, in their very silence alerted Triv and he glanced about him, startled. 'EV *is* coming back for us?'

'Despite Gaber's gossip, there's no reason to suppose not,' said Kai, slowly. 'Once EV strips the messages, they'll come rattling here. This planet is so rich in all . . .'

'Messages?' Triv caught Kai's inadvertent slip.

'Yes, messages,' said Varian, a sour grimace on her face.

'How many?' The geologist couldn't suppress his anxiety.

'The all-safe-down is the only one they've stripped.'

Triv absorbed that depressing admission with no hint of his inner reactions. 'Then we'll have to sleep.' He frowned and asked, as an afterthought, 'Only the all-safe? What happened? They wouldn't have planted us, Kai, there isn't a large enough gene pool.'

'That and the fact that we've the youngsters is what reassures us,' said Kai. 'I feel that the EV is much too involved in that cosmic storm and the Thek were of the same opinion.'

'Ah, yes, I'd forgot about that storm.' Triv's relief was

visible. 'Then we sleep. No question of it! Doesn't matter if we're roused in a week or a year.'

'Good, then we'll sleep tomorrow, once the others have been told,' said Kai.

Lunzie shook her head. 'Why tell them? Aulia'll go into hysterics, Portegin will insist we try to rig an emergency call, you'll get blasted for withholding information about EV's silence . . .'

'They're half-way there now,' said Varian, gesturing towards the sleeping forms. 'And we'll save ourselves some futile arguments.'

'And any chance of being found by the heavy-worlders,' said Triv, 'until either EV comes back for us, or the Thek arrive as reinforcement. There's no way the heavy-worlders could find a trace of us in cold-sleep. And there's a real danger if we remain awake.'

Such a major decision should be democratically decided, Kai knew, in spite of the fact that he and Varian as leaders could arbitrarily act in the best interests of the expedition. Lunzie's assessment of reactions was valid. Kai spread his arms wide accepting the inevitable. He'd given Tor a week which, if the Thek had been going to respond, would have been more than adequate for the creature to make the journey from the other planet. If Tor himself had received the message. It could have been taken by one of the other two, who would not necessarily pass it to Tor or bother about responding.

'I'd rather meet those heavy-worlders again with a healed shoulder,' remarked Varian. 'I hope they waste all their remaining power trying to find a trace of us.'

Triv gave a mirthless laugh and rose, looking expectantly at Lunzie.

'I'm not unusually spiteful,' said the physician, getting to her feet, 'but I'm of the same mind.'

Lunzie prepared a preservative which she then administered to the sleeping. Triv, Varian and Kai checked each one until their skins cooled and their respirations slowed to the imperceptible. Kai toyed briefly with the notion of staying awake, of asking Varian to join him in the vigil until either Tor or EV arrived. But that would mean they'd have to stay outside as the sleep vapour would permeate the shuttle. He'd no wish to remain away from his team and inadvertently to disclose their hideaway to the searching heavy-worlders. Soon the others were in the thrall of cold sleep.

'You know,' announced Varian in a startled tone of voice as she was settling herself, 'poor old Gaber was right. We are planted. At least temporarily!'

Lunzie stared at her, then made an unamused grimace. 'That's not the comfort I want to take with me into cold sleep.'

'Does one dream in cryogenic sleep, Lunzie?'

'I never have.'

'Seems a waste of time not to do something.'

Lunzie handed round the potion she'd made for them to take in lieu of the spray.

'The whole concept of cold sleep is to suspend the sense of subjective time,' she said. 'You sleep, you wake.'

'And centuries could pass,' added Triv.

'You're less help than Varian is,' muttered Lunzie and drank her potion, arranging herself.

'It won't be centuries,' said Kai emphatically. 'Not once EV has the assays on the uranium.'

'That is a comfort,' said Triv and drank his dose.

Tacitly Kai and Varian waited until the other two had quietened into the thrall of cold sleep.

'Kai,' Varian said softly, 'it is my fault. I had all the clues that pointed to a possible mutiny . . .'

'Varian,' he said gently and stopped her words of apology with a kiss, 'it was no one's fault, just a concatenation of forces. Content yourself that we are alive, so are they. Gaber brought his own end with an essential stupidity of temperament. And we had best suspend subjective time for a while.'

'How long a while?'

He kissed her lightly again, smiling a reassurance he tried hard to make genuine. 'EV will return for us. No matter how long it takes!' Not the most tactful remark to make. 'Drink,

Varian!' Raising his cup to her, he waited until she followed suit and they drank together. 'Nothing seems quite so bad when you've slept on it.'

'I hope so. It's . . . jussss . . .'

Silence pervaded the shuttle. The mechanism that released a vapour to reinforce the sleep opened the proper valve. All life-signs fell to an undetectable minimum.

Outside golden furred flying creatures roused with the advent of another gloomy, sultry Mesozoic morning.